THE BILLIONAIRE'S PLAYGROUND

RELUCTANT
BILLIONAIRE

Book Cover © 2020 Design by Tina Løwén

Editing by Lucas Cornelius
Proofreading by Abbie Nicole
Book Formatting by Tina Løwén

References to real people, events, organisations, locations, or establishments are only intended to give a sense of authenticity and have been used fictitiously.

The author acknowledges the copyrighted or trademarked status and trademark within the book.

Films, music, and lyrics *mentioned are the property of the copyright holders.*

Warning
Some of the content of this book is sexually graphic, with the use of explicit language and adult situations involving two males. It is only intended for mature audiences.

BOOKS BY THE AUTHOR

Standalone
When Fake Changed Everything
Christmas beyond Christmas
The Elves and the Bondage Daddy (Grim and Sinister
Delights Book 5)

Series
The Potters Creek Series
A Christmas Wish (book one)

The App Series
The App: Daddy kink (book one)
The App: Littles (book two)
The App: Puppy play (book three) - January 2021

The Flamingo Bar Series
Always More (book one)
The Little Side of Me (book two)
3 is the magic number (book three) – February 2021

La Trattoria Di Amore Series
Puzzle Pieces (book one)
Dominated but not Subdued (book two)

The Playroom Series
Mine, Body and Soul: Part One
Mine, Body and Soul: Part Two
Mine, Body and Soul: Part Three
Ferron's Journey: Damaged Part One (book four)
Ferron's Journey: Hidden Part Two (book five)
Ferron's Journey: Revelation Part Three (book six)
Mine, Body and Soul Trilogy

Ferron's Journey Trilogy

The Billionaire Playground Series
Property of a Billionaire (Book one)

The Manx Cat Guardians Series
Where it all Began: Origins (Book 1)
Seeing Beyond the Scars (Book 2)
Destiny Collides Past and Present (Book 3)
Searching for a Soul to Love (Book 4)
The 12 Disasters of Christmas (Book 5)
Laws of Attraction (Book 6)
The Teacher's Boy (Book 7)
Boxset

Audio Books
Mine, Body and Soul, Part One: The Playroom Series
Mine, Body and Soul, Part Two: The Playroom Series
Mine, Body and Soul, Part Three: The Playroom Series
Daddy Kink: The App (book one)
Always More: The Flamingo Bar (book one)
When Fake Changed Everything
Ferron's Journey: Damaged Part One
Ferron's Journey: Hidden Part Two

Story Outline

*Can a party, a rejection, and an interfering Nanna
help a reluctant billionaire find love, and the one
thing he craves most; acceptance for who he is?*

Brett Louden attends his best friend's engagement
party and finds someone to spark his desire. Only,
after a night of chemistry and a heated kiss, the much
younger man doesn't respond to his messages so he
gives up any hope he's interested.

That is until Brett is persuaded to go on holiday with
his family.

Guy Finchley is left at loose ends for the holidays, until
he's invited to Switzerland at the expense of his
friend's billionaire boyfriend. His life turns upside
down after he meets Brett again, and he is no longer
able to deny the attraction between them.
Unfortunately, Brett's father has other ideas about
what should happen between them. Will Nanna and
Guy be able to show Brett's father the error of his
ways while mayhem and disaster follow?

***Reluctant Billionaire (book two in the Billionaire's
Playground series) is a standalone, MM gay romance,
with a younger dominant man who has sass in bucket
loads and loves kick-arse heels.***

When you have a kick arse, amazing friend how can you not create a story for them? Thanks to Guy, for the inspiration and allowing me the freedom to write this book. Your input was invaluable ☺

PROLOGUE

Brett

As I slipped into the back of the Uber, I groaned aloud. The guy eyed me in the rear-view mirror but said nothing as he merged with the traffic to take me to the Flamingo Bar.

I loved Luke with all my heart, as a friend, but I'd admitted to myself I was jealous of what he had with Scott. They were so happy together, and this engagement party, though it filled me with utter joy for my best friend, left me green with envy. I'd always thought it would be me getting engaged first.

How did that turn out?

A stab of hurt pierced my heart and I rubbed at the centre of my chest. Ever since Nigel had cheated on me, then dumped me after five years being together, I'd admit to being floored. His comment that 'I was too out there for him' left me cold when I'd only experimented to keep things spiced up between us.

Luke had pointed out the fact that Nigel was a spineless dick, who'd shown his true colours in the end. That I'm a bloody doctor of psychology says I should have noticed how bad things had become between us. But no, I'd buried my head in the sand, to the point where I lost sight of what was happening in my own life.

Months had passed, and I was still struggling to get past it. The unsettling reality is that I was more upset by the fact I'd been duped than by Nigel dumping me.

I stared out of the window at the darkening sky and tried to distract myself with thoughts of what I'd find at this new kink bar. I'd tried many things over the years, hoping to keep Nigel interested, but nothing seemed to hold my attention for more than a few months before I'd be looking for something different to try.

You're supposed to be thinking about something other than Nigel!

The voice of reason did little to help settle my clenching gut, and by the time the car pulled up outside the large, converted warehouse, my mood had plummeted.

The warehouse was huge, consisting of three floors and an underground car park for patrons. The ground floor was a BDSM club called The Playroom that I'd never been in, but I was told it was a popular place for those interested in BDSM.

It was the next floor where I was headed. The Flamingo Bar was the newly refurbished part of the large warehouse. It was split into two, with a new restaurant in the La Trattoria Di Amore franchise and the kink bar. Carl, the head chef of the restaurant, was also the co-owner of the club below and the bar with Nathan. I'd not met either man as yet, though I'd heard good things about both of them from Luke and Scott.

Scott was the head waiter in the Flamingo Bar restaurant, and was also Luke's boy, which is why they'd decided to use this venue. The bar was geared to the lighter side of kink, Daddy kink, puppy/kitty play, age play, and any other kind of play imaginable.

In the empty lift, I leant back against the wall and inhaled a breath, then another, to help centre myself. I eyed my skinny trousers in deep brown that matched my snug-fitting jacket. The burnt orange shirt I'd paired it with was also fitted, and I sucked in my stomach when it poked out over my belt.

The door opened, and I was distracted from my weight gain by the scent of Italian food and expensive colognes. The room was an eclectic mix of reclaimed wood fittings and modern fixtures.

The handcrafted bar was beautiful, as were the booths that lined the walls, which also looked as if they'd been handcrafted. The dimmed lights that hung from recycled chains had different coloured glass bottles as shades, which cast coloured light over the tables in the booths.

"There you are, I thought you'd got lost," Luke exclaimed as he rushed towards me, looking more than a little flustered.

"Now, you know I like to make an entrance, honey." I puckered up my lips, and Luke rolled his eyes but gave in and pressed a quick, platonic kiss to my lips.

"Hey, what's this? I turn my back on you for two minutes and already you're kissing other men." Scott's eyes gleamed as he threaded his arm through Luke's and beamed at me, not looking in the least bit upset.

I offered my lips to him, "I'll happily give you a kiss too."

As he went to step forward, Luke held him back. "Nope, not happening. You kiss his sweet lips and you might get second thoughts about our engagement."

"As if, Daddy," Scott mock-whispered back, looking about to check no one was close.

Luke was still reasonably new to the Daddy scene, and though Scott wasn't, he was always mindful not to out Luke in front of his friends and work colleagues.

"Scott, have you got a moment? I need you to check you're happy with... something," asked a pretty guy dressed in a black shirt with pink flamingos on it.

"What's this about? You promised me you weren't going to be doing any work-related stuff tonight." Luke's brow furrowed as his gaze moved between the two men. "What gives Theo?"

"Luke, it's a secret," Scott stated in an exasperated tone as he rolled his eyes at Theo.

I chuckled when Luke got a twinkle in his eyes as he whispered something into Scott's ear, making his boy's cheeks fill with a flare of pink. Scott kissed his cheek before walking off with the other man.

"He looks so happy. I'm happy for you both." I glanced at Luke as he turned to stare at me.

"I know this is hard for you after—"

"Do not mention he who shall remain nameless. We're supposed to be having a good time." I swept my gaze around the bar before landing back on Luke. "Maybe I'll meet the man of my dreams tonight."

He laughed. "You know almost everyone that is coming tonight. Is there something you want to tell me?"

"Nope, but hope springs eternal." I sounded sad even to my own ears, so I offered him an extra bright smile, knowing it wouldn't fool him for a second but I had to try.

"I'm told Sam, the head barman, makes a killer cocktail. Let's go get one." Luke's eyes said that he was letting it go for tonight, but that he'd be having words with me at some point.

I threaded my arm through his and we went to the bar. He was right, Sam did make a killer cocktail. He was also a cute guy who liked to flirt. It didn't hurt my ego at all when he chatted me up and gave me a flirty wink before he went to serve someone else.

By the second cocktail, and having not eaten, I was starting to feel the nice floaty alcohol effects. I excused myself to use the bathroom, and on my return, Luke was no longer stood at the bar, but was talking to a number of men, including...Griffin Hudson, *shit*.

I got the feeling Griffin, who was exceedingly private, might find it difficult to see me after his last visit to my office. It happened from time to time when I was out and bumped into a client.

Unable to avoid the situation, I headed straight to the group of men. Walking up behind Luke, I wrapped my arm through his, giving everyone a bright smile. It was only then that I got a full look at the man stood next to Griffin's boyfriend Charlie. *Holy fuck!*

The wattage of my smile increased as my gaze travelled up his willowy frame. Thigh-length black leather boots were paired with super-skinny black jeans that made his legs appear as if they went on forever. The black fitted shirt had panelled mesh sides to show off his gorgeous body and made my mouth water. He was pretty, with blue-grey flecked eyes that showed a hint of uncertainty.

"Hello, sweetie, and who might you be?" I cooed.

Luke rolled his eyes and Griffin coughed, while the nameless man's face gained a beautiful rosy glow to it. His eyelashes lowered, and when he remained silent, I got the distinct impression that I might have embarrassed him.

Charlie nudged the man not so subtly and huffed as Griffin coughed again. "Hi, I'm Charlie. This is Guy, my best friend. And you are?"

I gave them both a big grin as I offered my manicured hand to Guy. "I'm Brett Louden, Luke's best friend...and Griffin's..."

I hesitated as Griffin stiffened next to Charlie. There was an awkward silence as I continued to hold Guy's hand, until I noticed Luke eyeing me. I reluctantly let go when Charlie spoke.

"It's nice to meet you, Brett, but I could really do with a drink. Guy, do you want a drink? Luke, Brett? Griffin and I can go to the bar."

Once Charlie had everyone's orders, they walked towards the bar, disappearing in the crowd. Luke glanced between me and Guy before he came up with some lame excuse and left too.

"How long have you been friends with Charlie?" I asked after searching for something to say to break the sudden tension rolling off Guy.

His face brightened. "Oh, since I started uni. We met in halls and ended up sharing a room. That was up until recently, he's moved in with Griffin now. But it's not too bad as we're in our final year." His slim shoulders shrugged as he glanced towards the bar, as if willing Charlie to reappear.

"That's how I met Luke. We lived together for four years." I wanted to slap my head when Guy's eyes widened and he looked over to where Luke stood with his arm draped over Scott's shoulders. A look of disappointment flittered over his face before his head moved and he looked back at me.

"Just as friend's, Guy, Luke is the brother I never had," I clarified, hoping I was reading him right.

When his lips moved into a beautiful smile, my heart thudded against my ribs. "Oh, right. You weren't ever an item?" he asked hesitantly.

"No, we kissed a couple of times when we were drunk." I chuckled. "It lacked any chemistry."

His eyes sparkled with humour. "That was like me and Charlie."

I linked my arm through his and gave him a sexy wink. "Then we already have lots in common. You want to find out what else we might have in common?"

Guy blushed but nodded as Charlie returned with our drinks.

Three hours later, feeling the effects of Guy's undivided attention and several cocktails, I pressed him up against the wall by the packed dance floor and kissed him.

His lips were soft, and he tasted of sweet alcohol as he allowed me to deepen and control the kiss. His slim body pressed firmly against mine, and his body's reaction became obvious as his cock pressed against my hip bone. The kiss ended all too quickly, when Charlie came to see if Guy was ready to leave.

Tempted to ask him back to mine, I instead offered him my number. After we'd exchanged digits, he left, and I went to the bathroom to make myself decent before I went to find Luke.

In the bathroom I couldn't resist sending Guy a text.

Thank you for making the evening extra special. I hope we can do this again soon, Brett x

I read it twice before I hit send. A smile plastered to my face, I went to find Luke, feeling the first flare of real happiness in months.

Six days later, the spark of happiness I'd felt at Luke and Scott's engagement party had fled. Guy hadn't answered my text, or the one I'd sent him three days earlier asking if he'd like to go out on a date.

I sighed and glanced at my phone, switching it to silent and putting it in my desk drawer before my next client arrived. I had a firm no phone rule in my office and that also applied to me. I hated that I'd broken the rule over the last three days, waiting like an idiot for Guy to reply. I'd gone over the evening, and I couldn't figure out why the radio silence. I'd reached out to Griffin to check nothing had happened to Guy. When he'd come back saying Guy was fine, my heart had sunk.

No more. It stops now!

It was his loss if he couldn't see what a great catch I was.

Really, then why are you single?
Oh, shut up!

CHAPTER ONE

Brett

I eyed my father across his large desk and met his hard stare with one of my own. Today's suit was charcoal grey and matched his hard, flinty grey eyes. The crisp white shirt he wore under the suit jacket had not one crease in it. He probably looked as immaculate as he'd done when he'd dressed several hours earlier. To him, it was unacceptable to look nothing if not perfect at all times.

We looked nothing alike, and I thanked the universe for that every time I looked into his cold eyes. I resembled my mother, pretty and delicate. My father was a hard-faced Russian, who cared more about money and status than family. I'd learned at an early age his beliefs about right and wrong were very different from mine. I firmly sat in the wrong column of the equation, and for that,

I'd suffered at his hands on more than one occasion.

It was a hard-won battle not to squirm under his stare, and I congratulated myself as I relaxed back in the seat I'd taken not more than five minutes earlier, after being summoned this morning. He wouldn't care that I'd had to move two client appointments to come and see what he wanted.

I'd given up years ago trying to justify why I still tried to please him, even though it meant nothing to him. "It's been months, to what do I owe the pleasure of a summons?"

His dark brow rose and his eyes glinted with anger. "We are spending the New Year in Switzerland with clients and their families, I need you to attend."

His Russian accent was thick, which told me he wasn't telling the whole truth. I'd spent years trying to figure him out, but all it had done was allow me to pick up certain cues. As for the rest of it, I'd given up because he never talked about his life in Russia, ever.

"Why do you want me to come? Normally you can't stand to be in my company for more than a few hours." I knew it was petty to point it out, but I couldn't help it. My father hated the fact I was gay. Hell, hate wasn't strong enough for what he felt about my sexual orientation.

18

"Your Mother has invited several friends and their families. It would seem odd if you did not attend."

"Again, why? You've never bothered about what others think, so why now?" I was heading towards forty years old, and not once had this man shown that he cared about anything other than money. This right here rang too many bells. He wasn't being honest with me and I wanted to know why.

He scowled and suddenly looked old, something I'd never thought about him before, given that he was only in his early sixties. He'd met and married my mother in a whirlwind romance when he'd come to England on business, only, he'd never left. He set up home here when my mother refused to go and live in Russia. It was the only time I think my mother had stood up to him.

"—have a gay son."

I blinked and sat forward, having missed the first part of what he'd said, but my stomach clenched at what I'd heard. "You're inviting me to help with a business transaction, aren't you?" I held my breath, hoping like hell I was wrong.

But when he didn't deny or confirm it, I sagged back in the leather armchair. "Why would I do this for you?"

"You're my son!" he answered indignantly, his accent becoming even thicker.

"When you want something from me, I am." I sighed as he shot me a challenging look.

"Who paid for the high-priced courses that got you your doctorate? Who gave you a trust fund that has set you up for life?" he gritted out through his clenched teeth, his face darkening.

It was an old argument. I'd not touched the trust fund, leaving it to a fund manager to take care of. A fund manager that had also wanted to meet today to talk about money, though I had no clue why.

Since I'd set up my practice ten years ago, I'd not touched a penny of my father's money. I had more than enough to live comfortably and afford my apartment in London. None of that mattered to my father because it meant he couldn't control my life the way he'd always wanted.

"You will come, if only for your Mother. She misses you."

It was a low blow, hitting my weak spot like that, and we both knew it. "Fine, but I'm only staying for a couple of nights."

His triumphant smile left a bitter taste in my mouth as I left his office and headed to my second, and last, appointment of the day. I trudged the dark streets of London, looking at the twinkling Christmas lights, finding none of the joy I normally felt for this time of year. The icy wind bit into my exposed cheeks as I hugged my wool coat to me and shoved my bare hands deeper into my pockets.

By the time I got to Steve Greenwood's office building, I was perished, and the mood I'd hoped to shift after giving into my father, held on. Stepping into the building, a shiver racked my body at the wall of warm air.

I kept my coat buttoned until I exited the lift and started to feel like I was thawing out. I was escorted into Steve's very warm office by his personal assistant, Freda. Steve thanked her and waited for her to shut the door before he spoke.

"Take a seat, you look frozen." His gaze moved to the large window behind him that overlooked the London Eye.

I took my coat off and sat in the chair facing his modern glass desk that held only a computer, several files, and a phone. Steve was in his late forties and had a round, friendly face that encouraged you to trust him. Underneath that exterior was a killer instinct and shrewd businessman.

"It's dry and there's no snow, but it's bitterly cold out there tonight. And I stupidly thought walking would be a good thing."

Steve's smile dimmed, he knew where I'd been before coming here, but he didn't mention my father. He picked up the file closest to him and handed it to me. "I'd like you to take a little look through this and then we can talk about why I've asked you to meet me."

My palms grew sweaty for no real reason as I took the file and flipped it open. I scanned the first and second page that highlighted transactions that meant nothing to me. It was only when I got to the last page that my brows shot up. I read the account figure four times before I glanced at Steve then back at the file I held. "This figure can't be right, surely?"

"It is, and if you need more clarification, I can have our accountants meet with you to go through all the figures."

"How can this be?" I licked my dry lips and struggled to count all the zeros.

"With the investments, interest, and your father adding to the fund every six months it's…grown."

"Grown?" I squeaked as I shot out of the seat and paced in front of his desk, my heart rattling against my ribs. "This is…fuck knows what you call it? Ginormous!"

"I suppose it is. Two Billion pounds is a substantial amount." He coughed as he finished talking, and I got the distinct impression he was amused by me, but I was still having an internal meltdown.

"I wasn't aware my father was still contributing to this fund! Why didn't you tell me? I could have at least stopped him."

Steve choked out a laugh. "This is your father we're talking about. When does telling him to stop doing anything ever work?"

My father was well-known in business circles all around the world. It was why I'd taken my mother's maiden name when I'd gone off on my own. I paced several more times in front of Steve's desk, not bothering to reply. The figure just kept going around on repeat inside my head. I was sure others in my position would be jumping up and down with joy, but me? I felt sick to my stomach with the responsibility for all that money.

"What am I going to do with it all?" I asked once I'd stopped pacing, failing to understand why my father continued to give me money.

"Spend some of it. There are a wealth of charities out there that could benefit and give you great tax benefits. It's why I called you in. With the amount growing quickly from investments and interest, I thought you might want to consider what you want to do with some of it." His forehead furrowed as his eyes narrowed on me. "Where the money currently sits, your father can access it. If you consider donating some to charities, then maybe now would be a good time to move the bulk of the money into your account from the trust account."

"If I move the money out, can we shut the trust account? Stop my father from accessing it?" Following Steve's mention of charitable donations, I was starting to see what some of the money could be used for.

There were several youth projects that could really benefit from large donations. I tapped my lower lip and, for the first time since I'd left my father, my good humour returned. My father wasn't the charitable sort, and only ever donated at my mother's insistence when they attended a charity event.

"As your father set up the account, I can't close it without his written permission, but you can move the money elsewhere as your name is on the account."

"Let's do that. That way I'll be able to control what it's used for without him sticking his nose in my business."

An hour later, I left Steve's office and hailed a cab to take me home. The smile was still on my face at thoughts of all the charities that were about to get a huge Christmas surprise.

CHAPTER TWO

Guy

"What do you mean you're spending the holidays with Chris?" I asked petulantly. I knew full well I sounded no better than a five-year-old, but I was pissed. Mum and I had always spent the Christmas and New Year holidays together, it had *always* been that way.

I don't know who my dad is and Mum never spoke about him. As far back as I could remember, there had only ever been the two of us. It had been a shocker to return home from uni this afternoon to find that the man my mum had met several months ago, wanted to take her on a cruise around the Caribbean.

"I know it's a little bit of a shock, Guy, but I didn't want to talk about Chris in a text message or on the phone, I wanted to talk about it face to face." Her eyes were sheened with tears and implored me to understand. I wanted to, but I felt like I'd been sucker-punched.

There was nothing we didn't talk about, nothing. She'd been my biggest supporter my whole life. When I came out to her when I was thirteen and not really sure what to do, she'd been there for me. It had been the same throughout all those firsts in my life, first kiss, first boyfriend, the first time I had sex, we talked about it all. This, on the other hand, felt like something she'd kept from me, and I wasn't prepared for it. She'd never dated seriously before.

"I'm…I don't know what I am. It's a shock, Mum." That was an understatement, but it was the best I could come up with.

There was a knock at the door, and my heart sank when Mum's face lit up in a way I'd never seen before. *She's happy! Really happy.*

The thought struck a chord in me when it was all she'd ever wanted for me. I sagged and blew out a huffed breath. How could I not want the same for her? "I'll get the door."

Her eyes widened, but she nodded and stood in the middle of the living room in the house that had been my home for all my life. My heart fluttered madly as I trudged down the small passageway to the door. Not giving myself a chance to brace, I opened the door and faced a man in his mid-forties.

The smile he wore dimmed as he met my gaze. He was attractive, with dark hair threaded with silver at the sides. He was dressed in casual trousers and a wool jumper, the logo of which marked it as designer and not cheap. He was several inches taller than me and much broader. He looked physically fit, and I knew damn well he'd laugh if I tried to threaten him.

That didn't stop me standing tall as I held out my hand. "I'm Guy, Reena's son." I waited a beat till he took my hand, then squeezed hard.

"You hurt her and I won't be responsible for what I do to you," I muttered, low enough for him to hear, but not my mum if she'd chosen to earwig.

His eyes lit with respect as he nodded. "I love Reena, and the last thing I want to do is hurt her, just for the record."

It was very unnerving to hear him say that, but I acknowledged the sincerity and tucked it away to think about later. Much later.

The following day, I waved my mum and Chris off, feeling at a complete loss. Chris seemed like a decent guy, and the way he fawned over my Mum, though uncomfortable to watch, left her glowing. Overnight, I'd come to the decision that if Chris could make mum happy, then I'd go with it, *for now.*

I shut the door on their grinning faces as the taxi drove them off to the airport for the first leg of their holiday.

What was I supposed to do now? I'd made no other plans because these were *always* my holiday plans. I sighed loudly and strolled back into the comfortable living room. Plonking myself down in front of the wood burner, I gazed at the flames, admitting I was lonely in the too quiet house.

My phone sat on the table and I lifted it, going to the messages I'd saved.

Brett: *Thank you for making the evening extra special. I hope we can do this again soon, Brett x*

Brett: *Would you like to go out for dinner? Drinks? Brett x*

The burning in my chest alerted me to the fact I was holding my breath. I'd not answered either message because I'd overheard Luke talking to Scott as we were about to leave the bar. Luke had said Brett was a mess over his ex-boyfriend dumping him. As much as I was drawn to him, I mean the man was stunning and intelligent, I'd done rebound guys before and it never ended well. So I'd not responded, thinking it was best for all concerned.

Then why have you kept his number and saved the messages?

It was a question I refused to answer, no matter how many times I'd asked myself. The screen lit up, and Charlie's number appeared.

"Hey, you are just the distraction I need," I answered before he could get a word in.

"Is that so? I'm ringing on the off-chance you want to do something different this holiday? Griffin has a work-related thing happening over the New Year in Switzerland, and I thought you might like to tag along. We could try our hand at skiing?"

"You know, it's almost like you and my mum have been in cahoots," I accused when Charlie sounded a little over the top, even for him.

He huffed and puffed down the phone. "I told her you'd figure it out! She's worried about you dwelling alone over the holidays. And my offer is genuine, Griff has work stuff in Switzerland. If you don't come you know Nanna will want me to teach her to ski or something equally horrifying," Charlie moaned.

Charlie's Nanna was a hoot. She had moved in with Charlie and Griff earlier in the year after she'd fallen and broken her hip. She was independent, and with Charlie's parents working, they'd all worried how she'd cope alone. So Griff had suggested they hire a nurse and she move into their new house in Brighton. Nanna had gone happily, and had loved it so much that Griff had built a granny annex for her and hired a chaperone.

"Give over, you love Nanna and her antics, it keeps you on your toes." I laughed when Charlie snorted down my ear.

"Not when those antics include her snooping in your drawers!"

This time I snorted, having a fair idea what was in the drawers she'd been looking in. "Okay, I'll give you that. There are some things you should never share with your Nanna."

"Anyway, we're getting off the subject, do you want to come? We're flying in Griff's jet. It will be a blast."

A smile formed on my face at the thought of travelling in such luxury for the first time. "I'm in. And I'll text Mum to tell her thank you."

"Hey, I was the one to offer you the holiday. Shouldn't I get a thank you too?" Charlie fired back through his laughter.

"Alright, sour puss, thank you too. Now, when are we leaving?"

There was a slight hitch in Charlie's breathing. "Can you be packed by teatime?"

"What? Are you serious?" I screeched. I needed at least a day to sort through what I'd need to take. I was a clothes whore, and as my major was fashion design, I liked to look my best if I went out anywhere, and Charlie knew this.

"Yeah, erm sorry about that. I was supposed to ring you last night, but Griff distracted me." Charlie did at least sound contrite as my heart skipped several beats.

"I'll see what I can do." I sounded anything but confident as I listened to Charlie explain what the plan was.

CHAPTER THREE

Brett

I refused to look at my father as the jet took off from Heathrow. He'd yet again managed to out manoeuvre me by sending my mother to tell me we had to leave a few days earlier than I'd agreed too.

In an attempt to keep from engaging in conversation with any of the other fifteen passengers on the private jet, I kept my gaze on the small window beside my seat. The flight wouldn't take long in the jet as there was none of the hoops others had to jump through. Luxury travel at its best, and I'd forgotten what it was like as I tended to avoid the ostentatious, extravagant lifestyle my father's money could afford us.

You can afford anything you want!

My stomach lurched and I glanced at my father, wondering what he'd think about all the charities I'd donated to. A perverse chuckle got trapped in my throat as his head turned in my direction. His hard, impenetrable stare met mine and his eyes narrowed before a man he'd not introduced me to asked him something and he glanced away.

Had he found out I'd moved all the money out of the trust account? I shook off the worry and glanced back out the window.

"Hello, are you Brett?" an overconfident voice asked, drawing my attention.

The man, who my senses told me was probably gay, stared at me like a bug under a scope. "Yes, I am. And you are?" His lip curled into an ugly sneer, as if I should know who he was. My skin started to crawl as he continued to stare at me.

"I'm Blake Masters, my father, Rupert"—he nodded in the direction of a rather pompous looking man—"is one of your father's investors." He made it sound like his father was somehow in charge of mine, which was laughable. My father had invested in some oil wells in Russia decades ago, and that was where the bulk of his money had come from. The rest was in areas he'd diversified into.

That was not what was concerning me though, it was how he knew who my father was.

Business was not something that interested me, and I tended to avoid any part in it, especially when it came to my father. So how had he made the connection?

I glanced at my father, who continued to talk to the man sat next to him. "It's not common knowledge who my father is..." I left the sentence unfinished as Blake flushed and his gaze finally shifted to somewhere over the top of my head.

"Oh I...I'm sure I've read it in some newspaper," he blustered, his lie more than obvious.

But for the life of me, I couldn't figure out what his game was, so I let it be and rather rudely dismissed him by looking back out the window. A headache was brewing at the thought of why I was actually here. Was my father trying to palm me off on this guy? He wouldn't? Would he?

He'd done some underhanded things in his time, but this? I wasn't sure this was his style. Or I hoped it wasn't. I sighed when Blake finally took the hint and walked back to his seat.

The next forty minutes felt like the longest in my life as I worked to keep a mask of indifference on my face while the horrible thought continued to niggle.

After exiting the plane in Zurich, I took a moment to breathe in the crisp, fresh air and release a little of the tension holding my back hostage. The process of going through customs was quick, and there were cars waiting to take us to St. Moritz. I'd have liked to suggest I go by train, on my own, but one look at my mother's face and I kept quiet.

It was only the stunning views out of the window that kept me entertained on the four-hour drive, trapped with my parents. My mother read one of her fashion magazines, whereas my father either worked on his palmtop computer or was on the phone.

When we eventually pulled up outside the stunning Grand Hotel, Des Bains Kempinski, next to the snow-covered Swiss Alps, my mood lifted.

As the car stopped, I was already reaching for the door to escape the feeling of oppressiveness my father tended to create inside me. A shiver of excitement raced through me as I eyed the snow-covered mountains. I'd learned to ski as a child, and I had never lost the love of the exhilaration that came from speeding down a mountain side in virgin snow.

"Brett? What are you doing here?" came an all too familiar voice.

I sucked in the icy air before I pivoted towards Griffin Hudson and my heart leapt in my chest. Stood beside him was Guy, the man who'd not answered my messages, and he looked gorgeous. His strawberry blond hair gleamed with gold highlights as the sun shone down on us. The thick ski jacket was a deep purple and flashed with white strips up the side. His ski trousers were black and matched the scarf around his neck. His eyes were shaded in a pair of Oakley sunglasses, making it hard to read his reaction at seeing me.

A smile, though forced, spread over my face as I offered my hand to Griffin as he led the men closer to the car. Oh fuck, my father!

How had I forgotten all about him? I blanched at the sound of feet approaching, right before I scented my father's aftershave. "Griffin, this is a surprise."

Griffin took my hand, but his gaze had already moved behind me. His eyes widened a fraction before he looked back at me with something like speculation in the depth of his eyes. We'd never talked about my family, and I could already tell that was about to change.

Guy was forgotten about briefly, while I released Griffin's hand and stepped back as my father stopped beside me. Resigned, I nodded towards each man as I introduced them. "Griffin Hudson, his partner Charlie McGregor, and Charlie's best friend Guy...this is my father, Maxim Pavel."

Guy didn't move his gaze from me, but he gave a kind of half-nod towards my father. It was Griffin's reaction that caused me the most distress. He'd evidently needed no introduction as my father was already offering his hand.

"I'm glad you were able to make the time over the holidays to meet and talk business, Griffin." My father looked at Charlie and his lips thinned, but he said no more.

Right at that moment, I cursed myself for the way I'd introduced Griffin and Charlie. I prayed I'd not fucked anything up for Griffin, if he was after doing business with my father. He never gave his opinion about how he felt about gay men, that was reserved for me because, in his eyes, that didn't count.

Griffin's eyes hardened, and he tugged Charlie into his side, making the relationship more than clear. "As I said, Maxim, I needed to pay a visit to the hotel and check up on the renovations." He glanced over his shoulder and a small smile graced his lips. "This was one of Alexander's favourite places to visit."

"Oh, there you are, I thought I'd lost you all," came a female Scottish-accented voice.

Before I could tilt my head to see around the group of men, Charlie groaned and spun around. "Nanna, wherever did you get to, we came out to search for you." There was clear exasperation in Charlie's tone as he placed his hands on his hips.

"Nonsense, Charlie boy, how can I get lost? I'm in Griffin's hotel, and the lovely lad on reception gave me a map to follow."

"You can't read a map, Nanna, you get lost in the supermarket!" Charlie muttered at the non-repentant Nanna, who was beaming at us all.

"Aren't you going to introduce me to all these gorgeous men? The one there at the end," Nanna pointed towards my father making him look behind him. I had to clamp my lips together to stop from laughing when she continued. "He looks like he could do with loosening up a bit. What's his name, he looks about my age. I'm sure he'd like a lady of my experience—"

Griffin groaned.

Charlie rolled his eyes, his face bright red. "Nanna, stop right there."

She didn't appear to hear Charlie as she walked to my father and held out her hand. The look on my father's face was priceless. I'd never seen him look flustered before.

"Hello, I'm Agnes, and you are?" She fluttered her eyelashes and offered what I'd bet she thought was a coy smile.

"Maxim Pavel, nice to meet you." His voice sounded strangled as Agnes pumped his hand and then winked at him.

"Do you know my Griff and Charlie boy? They get up to all sorts of antics, I bet you could be a naughty boy too."

Griffin sounded like he was choking, or was that my father? I wasn't sure.

But before she could say any more, Charlie took hold of her arm. "Come on, troublemaker. Mr Pavel, I apologise for my Nanna, she has no filter."

She snorted, but let Charlie march her back towards the entrance of the hotel from whence she came, but not before I heard her say, "I think Maxim will spice up my holiday. What do you think, Charlie boy?"

I couldn't make out Charlie's response as I tried to hide my growing amusement at my stuttering father. "That, yes...interesting...lady."

It was then I caught the glimmer of a smile on Guy's face, and I grinned at him, forgetting for a moment he'd rejected me.

CHAPTER FOUR

Guy

Glad that I was wearing my sunglasses, I'd worked to keep my shock hidden. *Brett was here! Brett was here on holiday!*

What was the universe trying to do to me?

I'd been in a dream state since I'd arrived in St. Moritz. The hotel was something out of this world. The food, the spa, the whole place was utter luxury and any pissed off feelings I might have had at my mum for going cruising and leaving me behind had fled the second I'd got on Griffin's jet. The whole adventure had been mind-boggling so far.

Christmas had been an experience when I was the guest of the owner of the hotel. All the joking I'd done with Charlie about how wonderful it would be to date a billionaire had been nonconceptual. The reality was so much more, and I'd admit I was a little jealous of Charlie because wow. Yet for all of that, I'd admit it was the way Griffin was with Charlie that really made me green with envy. The more time I spent with them, the more obvious how much they loved each other became. Charlie wasn't interested in what Griffin had financially. No, Charlie loved Griffin's big heart. To have that kind of love, yeah, I wanted that more than all the money in the world.

That, however, didn't stop me from admiring the rich people that floated about in a cloud of expensive scents. The first few days, I'd spent hours sitting in the lobby with my sketch pad, people-watching. Designer clothes gave me plenty to think about for the final pieces for my fashion show at the end of the year.

Then I'd spent some time with Nanna, which she insisted I call her when she found out mum's parents were dead. I'd vague memories of them, but my grandmother was nothing like Charlie's, who was a force of nature as she'd just proven by the little show that left Brett's dad looking shell-shocked and Brett amused.

As he smiled at me, I was reminded of kissing those soft lips of his, and my body heated. Something passed over his face, and the smile he'd just given me dimmed. I swallowed a sigh while I considered how to apologise for my dickish behaviour without revealing I'd not wanted to date someone who was on the rebound.

A pang of regret quickly followed, knowing I'd probably lost any chance of this gorgeous guy offering me a second chance. *You don't want to date a rebound guy, remember the last one!*

A shudder ran through me and I shoved the image of Nick from my mind.

With the heat of the sun baking my head, I felt sweat bead on my brow as I glanced around the front of the hotel, watching people come and go. Most were dressed like me, in ski suits to combat the cold. It was a strange concept, the snow and the heat of the sun.

I'd never been to Switzerland before, and I'd been surprised by the heat of the sun when it could still be so bitterly cold in the snow-covered mountains. The sun had given me a healthy glow over the last few days that made it appear like I'd been on a hot holiday. That was until I took my clothes off and the tan line stopped at my neck and wrists.

"Guy, could I have a minute of your time?" asked Brett.

I jerked, realising I'd zoned out and was now stood alone with him. When had the others left?

A flash of heat rode up my neck as I met his stare. Again, I was grateful for my sunglasses. "Okay," I replied, with a lot of resignation.

"I've never been at this hotel, could you recommend somewhere we can get a hot chocolate?"

Brett seemed genuinely keen on that idea and I responded with a big grin. "You're in for a treat. The Kempinski Bar makes the best hot chocolate I've ever tried."

The smile that re-appeared on Brett's face caused a flutter in my chest. To distract myself, I indicated for him to follow me. The front of the hotel reminded me of a Christmas card view, something too pretty to be real. I'd been over the moon to find I had a suite that overlooked the Swiss Alps, even though I'd hardly spent any time in it.

Once I'd found us a table, I beckoned a waiter to order for us. It was only when Brett gave me an amused smile that I realised I'd taken charge. Many of my friends, before they got to know me, had mistaken my fem appearance and need to please as a submissive nature. It couldn't be further from the truth, and though I could be submissive in the right circumstances, I preferred to call the shots. My choice of clothes, make-up, and shoes had nothing to do with my sexual preferences.

Recalling what Brett did for a living, I hoped he wouldn't try to analyse me. Would he think the lack of male figure in my formative years accounted for how I presented myself? Mum had been happy to let me find what worked for me and go with it.

Brett met my stare but, as I removed my ski jacket, his eyes slipped down my chest in the ribbed, thermal polo neck I'd put on to keep me warm. After slinging my jacket on the back of the chair, I sat and removed my glasses to place them on the round table between us.

He licked his lips, and I was again reminded of the kiss Brett had initiated. He'd taken control and, at the time, I'd let him, to see what he would do. A part of me suspected it wasn't what he preferred, but as I'd not taken it any further, I'd no way to know for sure.

The silence stretched between us, a tension building that caused a buzz of electricity to run through me.

"Why didn't you answer my messages?" Brett asked, his eyes widening as if he'd not intended to lead with that question.

"Truth?"

He nodded and shifted a little closer to me, his eyes lighting with something I couldn't fathom. My heart thudded against my ribs and I exhaled a shaky breath.

"I overheard Luke and Scott talking about how you were struggling with an ex-boyfriend dumping you. I've done rebound guys before and it's not great for anyone involved. I thought it was best to save us both from that. I'm sorry, it was rude not to message back." I was sorry, more than I wanted to admit, because the sexual chemistry I'd felt between us that night was still there.

"Oh, I see." He shifted and sat back. His face gave nothing away as a waiter approached with our drinks.

What did that mean?

When the waiter left, I eyed the creamy drink, then Brett's now dreamy expression with a chuckle. "It's an orgasmic experience, take it from me."

A pink-hue coated Brett's cheeks as his gaze moved to mine. "Let's hope so, it's been a long time since I've had one of those."

There was a vulnerable quality to his voice that left me yearning to...*what*? *You've rejected him.*

Brett picked up the glass by the handle, sniffed at its contents, and then took a sip that left a creamy smear on his top lip.

My mouth watered at thoughts of how the creamy sweetness would taste on his lips. "Good?" I asked a little breathlessly.

He grinned after he'd licked his top lip. "Hell yeah," he sighed dramatically. "I just know I'll not be able to resist having one of these every day, so that means I'll have to exercise."

The way he spat out the word exercise, like it was a dirty word, caused me to laugh as I looked him over. "You look great, and those extra calories won't change that."

He fanned his face with his free hand and fluttered his eyelashes. "Why, thank you, kind sir, but I've already got a muffin top because I indulge far too much and don't work out nearly as much as I—"

"Stop that. There is nothing wrong with you," I interrupted, sounding sharper than I'd intended. I took a breath before I continued, hoping to reign in my temper. "I'm sorry. It just annoys the hell out of me when people pull themselves down. We are all different, and what shape or size you are does not determine your worth as a person. I'm hoping one day to prove that designer clothes can show personality rather than an image that many will never attain in their lifetime."

It was my turn to blush as Brett's face glowed with something that tugged hard at my belly. "I hope you succeed. The world needs more designers to promote positive body images." He sighed. "I'm a doctor of psychology, you'd think I'd know better."

"It's hard, I'm sure, to apply it to yourself rather than pointing out issues to others," I said kindly.

"True." He took another sip of his hot drink and groaned. "This really is exceptional. However can I repay you?"

The thought that popped into my head got me lowering my gaze to my lap to check I wasn't going to embarrass myself in the busy bar. Appearing unaware of where my head had travelled, Brett carried on talking. "Have you been skiing before? Maybe I could teach you?"

"What a great idea," came Nanna's voice from behind me before I could answer. I twisted my head to see her grinning as if she'd just done me the biggest favour. "You could teach us both. Charlie boy said he would, but him and Griff have been too busy getting jiggy with each other. The sounds that come out of their suite would cause an avalanche for sure."

I groaned, not wanting to think about what my best friend got up to with his boyfriend. "Nanna, please, that's my best friend you're talking about."

Her brows rose up her forehead, deepening her wrinkles. "What? I've been looking on the interwebby and those sites show that gay men enjoy other gay men's exploits in the bedroom," she stated in a loud voice, causing several heads to turn and Brett to choke on the sip of drink he'd unfortunately just taken.

"Yes, well, maybe we could go back to talking about skiing," Brett spluttered out, and I gave him a grateful smile. "I'll happily teach you both. But Agnes, are you sure you'll be okay skiing?" he asked rather delicately.

Shit, I was going to kill Nanna! How was I going to be able to say no? *Do you want to say no?*

I acknowledged the part of me that wanted to spend more time with Brett as Nanna decided to take a seat next to him.

She patted his knee. "Don't be worrying your pretty little head about me. Griff bought these hip protector thingies to make sure I don't break my new hip, or the old one for that matter." She giggled as she glanced between the two of us with a look of triumph. It was then I recalled our first night in the bar when Charlie and Griff had gone back to their room. Nanna had pumped me for information about myself, and after I'd drunkenly confessed to wanting to find a boyfriend like Griff, she promised she'd help me, and I'd agreed.

Dear lord, what had I done?

I swallowed a groan of panic as it dawned on me that I'd been outmanoeuvred by a meddling Nanna.

CHAPTER FIVE

Brett

I wanted to kiss Agnes when, the next day, she gave me a valid excuse to avoid spending time with my family, showing up at breakfast to remind me of our plans.

"I'm so excited, Brett, you're such a sweetheart to offer to teach me to ski."

I didn't contradict her, knowing fine-well she'd painted me into a corner. I suspected she'd picked up that I liked Guy and was happy to have any excuse to spend time with him.

I'd given a lot of thought, last night after I'd gone to bed, to what Guy had said about Nigel. He was right. He could well have been a rebound boyfriend, but we wouldn't know that for sure. But I'd realised that I could turn this shit show my father had created into something fun.

Agnes beamed at me before she glanced in my father's direction. "Such a pity you're married, I'm sure we could have had so much fun, Maxim."

The expression on my father's face was about as stunned as my mother's. I smothered my laughter with a cough.

Evidently, my father hadn't mentioned what Agnes had said to him the day before. My mother eyed Agnes up and down. The ski suit she wore was a bold red and gave her a youthful appearance that belied the full head of silver-grey hair and wrinkles. Her sunny smile and dancing eyes added to the overall effect and I responded with a smile when she winked at me.

"You ready? I left Guy getting ready, the boy takes forever. He said he'd meet us in the foyer." She continued to chat, but I didn't hear another word as my father's eyes hardened at the mention of Guy's name.

Seeing this wasn't going to end without me getting a lecture, or into a fight I'd never win, I placed my napkin beside my half-eaten breakfast and stood, nodding to both of my parents. "I'm finished, have a good day. I'll maybe see you later, but don't organise anything for me as I don't know what time I'll be back."

"Brett, a word."

It wasn't a request, but before I could reply, Agnes linked her arm through mine and gave my father a stern look. "Maxim, I'm sorry, but we can't hang around all day chatting. There are slopes to be conquered." With that, she tugged me away from the table with more force than I would have expected.

In the foyer she stopped and looked back, as if to check my father hadn't followed, before she whispered, "I know he's your father, but he needs to take the stick out of his arse and live a little." She gave a dramatic sigh. "I could've helped, but alas, he's married and I don't poach."

Belly laughter I couldn't hold in poured out just as Guy exited the lift, looking spectacular dressed all in black. His sunglasses swung from his fingers as he walked over to us with an air of confidence that left me feeling hot under the collar.

"Nanna, what have you done now?" asked Guy as he stopped in front of us, and I wiped at my damp eyes, regaining my composure.

"Why nothing. I just said Brett's dad needs to live a little is all." Agnes gave Guy a beaming smile that didn't fool anyone for a second.

"I bet that is only the half of it," he said, shaking his head as he glanced at me. "I'm betting it was more what she could do to your dad, right?"

I snorted and struggled to contain another bout of laughter. "You hit the nail on the head. How did you guess?"

"I've spent the last few days learning that when Charlie says Nanna has no filter, he means it." Guy gave Agnes a smile before he glanced about the foyer. "Is anyone else joining us on the slopes?"

There was something about the way he asked which caused me to question if he'd changed his mind and didn't want to spend the day with me. "No, it's just us. That is, unless you want me to get you a proper instructor?" I added on the latter, reluctantly, when his brow furrowed.

"Oh, right. Aren't you here to spend time with your parents over the holidays?"

His gaze met mine and I swallowed to wet my mouth. "My father is here purely for business and nothing more." The truth came out before I could think better of it, and Agnes's and Guy's brows arched. "He's very work focused...I was only invited to...well, I'm not quite sure why." I shrugged, while heat surged up into my face. "Shall we get going? We'll need to get to the ski shop to hire our equipment and get our passes."

"Erm...we'll only be doing the novice slope, right?" Guy asked with alarm.

Happy for the distraction from my shitty family, I grinned at him. "Of course. I'll take you to the *baby* slope," I joked.

Agnes harrumphed and narrowed her eyes at me. "Less of the baby slope, we'll use the Nanna slope if you don't mind."

"Just take us to a slope that won't make us look like fools, okay?" Guy muttered as he headed to the door.

We followed behind and my gaze drifted down to his backside as it swayed seductively. The first night we'd met, I'd been entranced by the way he walked in his thigh-high boots. Even in flat boots, he had a sexy walk.

Agnes's elbow connected with my rib. "I bet you could bounce a coin on that arse."

"Agnes, really," I choked past my laughter and mortification at being caught. "I was…"

"Admiring that fine bottom," she gave a dramatic sigh and whispered in my ear, "you pair will make a great-looking couple…naked."

I halted mid-stride, causing the man behind me to sidestep to avoid colliding with me, as my mouth hung open and I lost the ability to talk. Had she just said that? Agnes's unrepentant smile clearly said I'd heard correctly. I pointed at her, "You're so bad."

"I know, but what's the point in being good when I have so little time left?" She didn't sound resigned, but more philosophical.

"I suppose you have me there."

"Are you pair coming?" Guy questioned from the entrance to the ski shop, his voice sounding a little impatient as his eyes narrowed on Agnes.

Was he in a rush to get the day over? I hoped he wasn't as we walked to him and I gave an apologetic smile. "Agnes was being...Agnes."

Guy glanced at the angelic smile on her face and rolled his eyes. "That look doesn't work on me anymore, Nanna. I'm not going to ask what you were talking about because I'm sure I don't want to know." His voice was laced with humour as he winked at me.

A flutter developed in the pit of my stomach. God, he was sexy.

The door in front of us opened, and I stepped aside to let the couple pass. Guy seemed to take a deep breath as he walked in through the door I'd taken hold of. Agnes followed, and we spent the next hour getting kitted out.

By the time we were on the slope for beginners, both Agnes and Guy looked a lot more relaxed.

I kept my attention on them both and ignored the laughter of the children and few adults around us that were being taught how to ski. "Right, a few things to get in your head before we start. Skiing isn't a sport that takes an hour to learn, it takes a lifetime of practice, so don't worry if you don't get to grips with it straight off. Very few people are natural-born skiers.

"The number one lesson on our list is learning to squat, you need to have a bent knee." I demonstrated and was pleased when both Guy and Agnes followed suit and copied me. "A lot of the time you'll be tempted to straighten your legs, but it messes up your form, balance, agility, and control. Bending your knees does a number of things. It forces you to shove your shins into the front of the boots, gaining control of your ski. Like this," I gave them a quick demonstration and moved slowly over the small slope.

Agnes whooped and cheered while Guy looked impressed as I side stepped back up the tiny slope to them. "Did you see how it helped to centre my upper body above my legs, keeping my balance?" When they both nodded, I continued to repeat the move until I felt confident that they'd understood how vital it was.

"How do you know you're bending your legs enough?" Guy questioned, his eyes hidden behind ski goggles.

"As long as your heels remain in the heel cup in your boot, then you know you have enough bend in your leg. If it doesn't sit in the heel, then you're probably not bending your knees enough."

"Cool, that's easy to remember, right, Nanna?" Guy grinned at Agnes, and for the first time since we'd started, he sounded genuinely excited.

"I don't know about that, my thighs are already starting to ache," Agnes complained, with a smile.

We'd been at it for an hour, and I considered suggesting we take a break, when she asked, "What's next?"

"We learn to fall because you'll end up doing it a lot. As a beginner, you won't be going too fast and snow is softer than you'd expect, but falling is a part of what you need to learn to avoid hurting yourself. We want to aim to fall to your side versus forwards or backwards. This will help you avoid twisting something vital. If you fall, self-arrest yourself so that you don't slide down the slope and either run into or over something." As I continued, they looked at me like I might have lost my marbles, so I pointed to the group off to our left as the ski instructor demonstrated falling. "See, it's all part of the fun."

Guy's eyebrows disappeared up under his ski hat. "Fun? Falling over in wet snow? Erm, I'm not sure about that."

Agnes gave Guy's back a playful slap. "Just think, falling at Brett's feet could be fun, when he gets to help *you up*."

The innuendo was there, but I refused to touch it as Guy shook his head, his already flushed cheeks darkening further.

"You're…words fail me," Guy huffed.

"Yes, I know, but I'm right." Agnes made a shooing motion at me. "Show how we have to fall because I for one don't need another broken hip."

The rest of the day was spent teaching them the basics. By the time we returned to the hotel, we were wet and exhausted. Having not skied in over a year, my leg muscles ached, but I couldn't remember a day where I'd laughed so much. Agnes seemed to act like a buffer between Guy and me.

She'd gone and sat for a little while and had laughed at our antics. The cloudless sky and bright sun had added to the overall lightness of the day while we'd acted like children, playing in the snow.

But now we were back in the bar having a hot chocolate, I wasn't sure of my moves. I'd always been the assertive one, but somehow, even though Guy was much younger than me, it felt different with him. Should I ask if he wanted to go to dinner with me? The sting of his last rejection had faded with the understanding of why he'd done it. That still didn't tell me if he was interested in more.

I swallowed a sigh and distracted myself by listening to Agnes.

CHAPTER SIX

Guy

"That's me, I'm done in. I need a hot bath and a lie-down before I get my glad rags on for dinner." Nanna gave me a look I struggled to understand until she nodded towards Brett none too subtly.

"What are you doing later, Brett?" I asked, hoping he'd not think about my previous rejection.

"I've no specific plans, why?"

His mouth pinched and there was a little strain about his eyes that caused my pulse to throb in my neck.

"Do you want to join," I glanced at Nanna then back at Brett when she widened her eyes, "us for dinner?"

Nanna sighed dramatically. "Not *us*. Dear lord, how does anyone ever date these days with all this pussyfooting about?"

Brett laughed. "I'd love to join...whomever—"

"There you are, Brett, I've been ringing you for the last hour," Maxim stated harshly as he came to a standstill besides Brett's armchair. His face was unsmiling as he towered over the table. The aura of power that came off him was a little intimidating.

Brett's smile disappeared, and the air seemed to go from warm and inviting to frosty as fuck.

Maxim gave me a fleeting look before he dismissed me. The smile he gave Nanna at least held a little more warmth than the freezing arctic.

"I explained at breakfast I was going to be busy," Brett clarified patiently, as if he were speaking to a stroppy teenager.

Maxim appeared not to have heard him as he continued, "I've dinner plans with Griffin and several other businessmen this evening. I've reserved a place for you."

"Good for you. I'm sorry to say, I'm having dinner with Guy and Agnes." He sounded anything but sorry, and I started to get the feeling that Brett didn't get on with his father.

The atmosphere seemed to become charged as both men stared at each other, neither appearing to back down.

"Oh now, dinner with you, Maxim, sounds like something I'll enjoy. You never mentioned your wife, will she be joining us?" She got up and linked her arm through Maxim's. The anger I'd seen spark in his eyes turned to shock as he glanced down at Nanna. "I'd love to learn a little about what part of Russia you're from. I visited once, with my no-good husband."

I bit my lower lip as Nanna maneuvered Maxim towards the bar exit as she continued to talk at him. I grinned at Brett. "How long do you think it will take for him to realise he's been outsmarted by Nanna?"

He rubbed at his face before he eyed the door they'd gone through and then looked at me. "I'd say maybe five minutes. But as I don't want to be here to find out, I'm going to head up to my room."

Unsure what possessed me, I stood and lifted our half-finished drinks. "Want to come back to my room, he won't find you there?"

The smile that lit Brett's face was stunning, and the room seemed to fade into the background. All I could see was the way he was looking at me, his eyes full of gratitude. The urge to put the glasses down and take hold of him and kiss him was so strong, it left me dithering for long seconds while he stood and waited for me to move.

I licked my dry lips and sucked in a shaky breath while I turned to walk out of the bar through the other door that exited near the lifts. I checked the hallway before I darted to the lift as it dinged. A group of people exited in a cloud of expensive scent. I glanced back at Brett, who was searching the corridor.

"Quick, get in before we get caught," I encouraged as I stepped into the lift, careful not to spill our drinks.

He followed suit and his finger hesitated over the buttons for the floors as he glanced at me. "What floor?"

"The fourteenth, I'm in suite fourteen-twenty."

Brett's eyes widened and he chuckled before he looked at the panel and pressed the button. "I'm in fourteen-twelve, we're almost neighbours"

Was that excitement in his voice? I wasn't sure, but his smile appeared to brighten. Although that could have been due to the lift doors shutting and our successful evasion of his father.

I ignored the pang of disappointment at that idea and handed over his glass. "Here, this definitely tastes better hot."

He took the glass. "It's chocolate, hot or cold it's all the same to me." He sipped at the drink and groaned, his eyes fluttering closed.

"You really like chocolate?" There was a breathless quality to my voice as his eyes opened and as our gazes connected. I forgot what I'd said for a moment, as a vulnerability he couldn't conceal fleetingly flooded his eyes before the confident man that he portrayed to the world returned.

The urge to kiss him returned, and I stepped closer to him, keeping hold of his gaze, showing him my intention. He seemed to hold his breath as I carefully moved the arm holding his glass to his side, while being mindful of mine in my other hand.

I pressed my chest against him and moved my mouth to his until they were almost touching. His nostrils flared as his eyes widened, but he never moved, and my cock pulsed with arousal. "Can I kiss you?" I murmured softly against his lips.

His eyes blinked owlishly.

"Yes." The whispered reply brushed against my mouth as his chocolatey-sweet breath mingled with mine.

Slowly, I traced the seam of his lips with my tongue until his mouth opened and I could deepen the kiss. His body vibrated against mine, and in the small confines of the lift, I could scent his aftershave and sweat from the day's exertion.

A low moan rumbled through him as I swept my tongue deeper into his mouth, wanting to taste him. His struggle to remain submissive became obvious as his lips firmed and he made a move to push me back against the wall.

Chest heaving, I released his mouth and shook my head. "No, sweets, I'm in charge, not you." As I spoke, I pushed my lower body firmly against his, pressing hard on his arousal with my own as it bucked at my words. "I'm getting the sense you've always been in charge in the past, but," I nipped at his lower lip, "if you're interested in taking this further, you should know something about me."

Again I nipped at his lower lip, only this time, I sucked the swollen flesh into my mouth to soothe the sting. "I prefer to top. I love nothing more than to wear my kinky boots and fuck my man into the mattress."

"Oh fuck," Brett cried out as he pushed against me, just as the door opened.

There was the sound of a cough and a muffled giggle. Knowing there was no way to pretend we'd been doing something else, I twisted around, hoping my ski trousers hid how aroused I was, and smiled sheepishly. "Oops, sorry about that, but my guy is just too cute to resist."

There was an indrawn breath from behind me, which I ignored for now, as I faced a man and woman in their fifties. They were dressed for an evening out or a night in the hotel casino. The woman eyed us both with more interest than the man as I tugged a frozen Brett out of the lift.

"Have a lovely evening," I muttered as we passed them, and I marvelled at how we'd not spilled a drop of our hot chocolate on the marble floor.

Only when I'd shut the door of my suite did I let out my laughter. "That could have been very hard to explain if we'd got caught by Charlie and Griffin."

Brett, who'd been moving to the sofa, stopped and turned to face me, the colour fading from his cheeks. "Oh, you don't want them to know...we...what..." he trailed off, his gaze dropping to the floor in front of him.

My stomach quivered at how insecure he sounded, and I walked to him after placing my glass down. "Know, we, what? I'm not sure what you mean, sweets."

His brows arched before he placed his own glass down and ran his hands through his styled hair, making it stand up all over the place. "The kiss. You don't want anyone knowing about...that?" he asked hesitantly, appearing to avoid any reference to more.

Did he think I wanted to hide? I went over what I'd said. "*Shit*, do you think I meant I was bothered at either Charlie or Griffin knowing about us?" His head moved in acknowledgement and my heart plummeted to my feet.

Fuck's sake!

"That couldn't be further from the truth. I was more concerned about them seeing you aroused and removing the choice from you." As I was watching him carefully, I didn't miss how his eyes misted over and his lips quivered.

Unable to resist the urge to comfort him, I took hold of his hands and tugged him to me. He came willingly, so I released his hands and wrapped mine loosely around his waist. At around the same height, I easily met his gaze. "Now we've cleared that up, I believe we were interrupted in the lift before you could give me an answer."

A look of confusion crossed his face and I grinned at him, pressing my lower body closer to his. His arousal had waned, but I hoped to change that. I gently kissed him as I dropped my hands lower, to clasp his plump backside. Groaning at how fleshy it was, I dug my fingers in, imaging sinking my teeth into the round globes. Any hopes of keeping the kiss light disintegrated as Brett's body reacted to my touch.

His lips parted, and this time, he didn't attempt to take back control. The moans and whimpers he released into my mouth were intoxicating. His whole body appeared to go pliant, allowing me to dominate him. "Such a beautiful, sweet baby, I could eat you whole," I mouthed against his hungry lips.

"More, I need more," he whimpered as he tugged at the layers I'd worn for skiing. His face flushed and his chest heaving, as his eyes begged, making it hard for me to keep control.

His whole body quivered, and he cried out as I rocked my hips against him, mimicking fucking him. "You haven't answered me, sweets. Are you okay with me being in charge?" I kept up the rocking and grinding as he looked at me with a dazed expression.

"Ugh, what...yes...anything, just, don't stop," he pleaded in such a way I wasn't sure we'd not end up naked before the night was over. Did I want just a quick fuck? The day I'd spent with him had shown another side to the flirty man I'd first met. He was kind, considerate, and above all, patient. He'd had to be with Nanna and me when neither of us had turned out to show any real finesse for skiing.

I sucked in a shaky breath, then another when it registered I didn't want just a quick fuck. I wanted...more. His pouty lips were too hard to resist, so I gave him one long lingering kiss, teasing us both until we were breathless, before I took a step back.

"What...why are you stopping?" Brett panted as he registered the distance I was putting between us.

I licked my lips and swallowed hard. "Sweets, if we don't stop now, I'll have you bent over the back of that very posh sofa—"

"I don't see a problem with that."

I chuckled at his crestfallen expression when I remained where I was. "That may be so, but I don't want a quick fuck. I want...to date. To take you up on the offer you once made me, only with a difference. This time when it comes to sex, I'll be the one in charge."

He shivered and his hand went straight to his cock. His eyes pleaded, even when he got a dreamy look at my offer to date. I gave his hand a pointed look, and I was rewarded when it dropped back to his side without him saying a word. "You want to date me?"

I nodded. "That's what I want. Are you over your ex?" The air remained stuck in my lungs as I waited to see what his reply would be.

He didn't answer straight away, and it helped settle my nerves, knowing he was giving his answer some thought.

The seconds stretched as his expression became thoughtful. "Nigel and I were together for five years. I wasn't prepared for his betrayal, or that I'd chosen to ignore the signs that things weren't right between us." He rubbed at his chin, his eyes sheened with tears. "It was a bitter pill to swallow and the taste lingered for a lot longer than I'd hoped it would. You probably saved us both all those months ago by not answering my text message, but I'm ready to try...something different."

CHAPTER SEVEN

Brett

The brush of icy air against my cheeks was thrilling as I skied to a halt at the bottom of the beginner slope. It was day three of teaching Guy and Agnes to ski and it was also New Year's Eve. The days seemed to fly by, and I was not looking forward to having to leave in two days' time.

It had felt like Guy created a little bubble around us that allowed me to just let go of any expectations and have fun. I couldn't remember the last time I'd been able to stop my father's behaviour impacting on how I felt. *Maybe that's because you've avoided him?*

With the excuse of spending time with Agnes and Guy on the slopes, I'd only had to endure one meal, the night before. That I'd invited Guy to dine with us had gone down like a lead balloon, but I'd not given my father a chance to refuse.

Unfortunately, the dick from the plane, Blake, had been present, and had spent all night giving me odd looks that had Guy bristling with temper. My heart fluttered in my chest at how he'd made his point to Blake that I was with him. The kiss had all but blown the top of my head off and given my father a face that resembled a beetroot. We'd made a quick exit after the meal, and gone to Guy's room where he'd proceeded to kiss me until I couldn't remember to be worried about how Father would react to me being kissed so publicly.

I'd been more than a little disappointed we'd stopped, again, after the kissing part of the evening. Guy was really good at the tease, and I was more than ready to beg after spending three days with blue balls. There was an unspoken rule that I would not find my release without him. It was there on his face every time I left his room, the demand I let him take the lead.

It had left me edgy, but in all my searches for something more to spice up my sex life, I'd never found this level of excitement that lasted for days. It was there when I woke up and when I went to sleep. My dreams were filled with erotic moments that both tortured and pleasured me in equal measures. Guy's whispered words about how he was going to pleasure me ran through my mind constantly.

I clamped my thighs together and glanced down quickly, releasing a relieved breath it wasn't obvious where my head had gone. With the number of small people around me, the last thing I wanted was to be accused of something nasty.

Shaking off the worrisome thought, I glanced back up the slope to where Guy and Agnes stood next to each other, having a conversation. Agnes's snow suit stood out against the pure white snow. It was canary yellow, with black stripes up the sides that made her resemble a bumble bee. Guy, on the other hand, had gone for a pale aqua suit that showed off his tanned face. He'd complained about the goggle marks when he'd taken them off the day before and he had a tan line. Agnes had informed him it made him look interesting, though Guy hadn't quite seen it like that as I recalled.

 When Agnes nodded at me, I held my breath as she started to glide down the slope at a snail's pace. Each and every time she came down, I went through the same panic I'd felt after Charlie, when he'd found out I'd offered to teach her, had threatened to chop my balls off if Agnes fell and hurt herself.

She was never going to be the best skier, but what she lacked in skill she made up for in enthusiasm. I released the breath I'd held as she stopped within inches of me, looking very pleased with herself.

She lifted up her goggles. "I think that was the best run yet," she gasped breathlessly, her eyes sparkling as she glanced up at Guy and waved at him.

As I shifted my gaze back up, my heart thudded painfully against my chest at the sight of the child that was off to Guy's left who had lost control and was aiming for his back. I knew it was too late as the shout left my lips. "Watch out."

Guy wobbled as the child's ski hit his, then he lurched forward. Instead of attempting to stop himself with his ski poles, Guy shot forward faster than he was used to. His eyes were masked by his goggles, but his lips were moving. My hands gripped my ski poles as I watched helplessly as he careened towards a group of children. I thought I heard him cry as he tried to shift his weight and ended up tumbling forward. Then it all seemed to go in slow-motion as Agnes cried out and Guy landed in an awkward heap ten feet from us, not moving.

"Guy! Guy? Fuck, are you okay?" I shouted as I sidestepped up the tiny bit of hill towards his unmoving body. One of the instructors made it to him first, and I watched him take off his glove and go to Guy's neck.

Nauseous, my guts churned as it seemed to take forever to reach Guy. A crowd was gathering, and I could hear Agnes behind me ask someone to take off her skis.

But my focus was on Guy, and by the time I got to him, my chest was burning and I felt like I'd climbed Mount Everest. The instructor had pushed his goggles up his forehead, but his eyes were shut. "Guy, baby, open your eyes for me," I demanded in a strained voice.

It was only when his eyelashes fluttered open that I took a breath. His blue-grey eyes met mine and a smile formed on his lips. "Well, so much for learning to fall."

I bent to release my skis so I could kneel next to him as the instructor started to ask him if anywhere hurt.

"Only my ego, I think. My wrist aches a little, but more like when you twist it and get a strain." His face was a little pale as he sat up and tugged his goggles off. He raised his hand and touched my cheek. "I'm okay, are you? You look a little pale there, sweets."

He gave me a beautiful smile as he continued to touch my cheek, and I struggled to answer him past the relief he was fine and the exhilaration of his touch.

Then there was a voice I'd rather not have heard boom out, "What happened here?"

I groaned as I glanced over my shoulder at my father. He was dressed for skiing, all in dark blue, as were the group of men that were with him. His expression was hard and unforgiving as he glanced between me and Guy. Instantly, my back went up, and I gritted my teeth to control the anger fizzing inside me. "Guy was knocked over by someone who lost control. *He's fine*." I stressed the last part, knowing it would be the last thing he'd have asked.

His eyes narrowed on me before they moved to the hand Guy had on my arm. "I'll see you in my suite at six-thirty for pre-dinner drinks." He gave me no time to reply as he skied off.

Agnes pressed her gloved hand onto my shoulder. "Don't mind him, he'll come round."

I didn't look at her as I answered. "He's not come around yet, I think hell might freeze over first," I stated dejectedly.

"We'll see about that," Agnes muttered, but I didn't argue with her.

What was the point when I'd had to live with his disapproval for decades? Nothing had changed it, no matter how much I wanted him to see me and love me for who I was.

I plastered a 'nothing to see here' look on my face as I helped Guy up, once assured he'd not broken anything.

With the skiing lesson over for the day, I left Guy and Agnes in the bar drinking hot chocolate to return to my room to shower. Well that was what I'd told them, but in reality, I'd needed a moment to pull myself together. I was sure it had taken years off my life when Guy had fallen.

It was the depth of my feelings that had shaken me. At the time, father had distracted me, but when we'd come into the hotel and several people had asked Guy if he were all right, I'd realised just how serious it could have been.

What if he'd broken his neck?

A shudder ran down my spine as I exited the lift, distracted by my thoughts. I didn't notice Father stood outside my room until it was too late to escape. As I met his hostile stare, I realised my error in coming up alone. With nowhere to hide, I stood taller and masked my thoughts as I walked to him. When I stopped beside him, I made no attempt to open my hotel room door.

"Father, is there something you need?"

"A word, Brett, in private. You've been avoiding me for days. I asked you to come with your mother and me to spend the holidays together—"

I held my hand up to stop him. "Please, you know that's not true. You've spent the last three days doing business. Mother has been skiing with the wives of your business acquaintances. And if you'd taken the time to ask Mother, she'd have told you we've spent time together every day." I called his bluff, pissed off that he was yet again laying the blame at my door for his own shortcomings.

Mother had made friends with Agnes because, how could she not? After the first day, Agnes had talked my mother into coming to sit with us after we'd finished skiing on the beginner slope. It had set the pattern for the last couple of days.

His dark brows arched, but his expression remained the same. "Open the door and let us go in so we can talk in private."

My pulse thudded in my ears as I faced him head-on. "No, if you have something to say to me, say it, then leave."

He seemed to grow taller as he towered over me, and I struggled to continue to hold his gaze. The anger was clear, but for a moment, I thought I saw disappointment before it was gone. Thinking I must have imagined it, I braced for the anger.

"Last evening, then again outside, you let that man touch you in public."

His Russian accent butchered the words, but I got the gist. "Yes, and your point is what? He's my boyfriend, why wouldn't I let him touch me, or want to touch him? You touch Mother in public. I never call you out for it." I hated that my voice didn't sound at all assertive, but I was pleased I'd managed to get the words out.

His face was again an ugly purple, and I was sure there was steam coming out of his ears. "You will rectify your behaviour in public or suffer the consequences," he growled threateningly.

I tilted my head back a little. "Rectify my behaviour in public? Or what, you'll ground me? Father, you have no control over me, and haven't for many years."

"Is that so? I can close your trust fund and take away the additional income you've happily been living off." He didn't mince his words, and they sliced deep, but not because they were true. Just the opposite in fact. That he had no idea I was so successful in my own right left me gutted. It took all my effort not to sag under the weight of how little he knew about my life.

"Go ahead." It was a struggle to say those two words, with the ball of tears wanting to choke me, but I managed to get them out.

Ignoring him, I pulled the key out of my pocket and froze when I caught movement out of the corner of my eye, halfway down the hallway. I didn't need to look because my gut already told me who was standing there. How much had they heard?

CHAPTER EIGHT

Guy

With nowhere to escape, I swallowed the sigh when Brett shifted, and I knew he'd seen me. I'd a feeling I'd heard most of the conversation. Maxim had been in no way quiet.

It was the devastation in Brett's voice that had caused me to walk towards them, unsure what I was going to do until I reached his side. I slid my arm around his waist, not overthinking how he'd declared to Maxim we were boyfriends. I wanted to talk to him about that in private, so I gave Maxim a smile that didn't reach my eyes. "You do know that you aren't living in the cold country anymore? Or has that slipped your mind?"

Brett stiffened in my hold, but he didn't pull away as I continued to hold Maxim's hard, hostile stare. If this were what Brett had to endure for years, I was surprised he'd turned out to be so well-adjusted.

"Who do you think you're talking to?" Maxim ground out in a thick Russian accent.

I sucked in a shaky breath. "An ignorant arsehole, that's who. A man who doesn't deserve to have a son like Brett." Building a full head of steam, I didn't let him get a word in. "A man who uses bullying tactics and threats to get what he wants, instead of love and care. Your son deserves the latter not the former. Now if you'll excuse us, I want to give my boyfriend the loving attention he deserves." I took the key card from Brett's white knuckled hand and pushed it into the lock, pleased when the green light appeared immediately.

"Brett—"

"No, you don't get to talk to him unless it's to apologise." I gently nudged Brett into his room and firmly shut the door in Maxim's shocked face.

Once the door was locked, I glanced at Brett, who looked a little green around the gills. Shit, had I overstepped? Recalling my harsh comments, my stomach knotted. I'd not had a father, so I had no gauge as to how I'd feel if someone decided to dress mine down.

"I'm sorry—"

"Please don't apologise," he sobbed, right before he wrapped his arms around me and held on.

His whole body shook, and his sobs were muffled as he buried his head in my neck. I held him and made gentle shushing sounds. His chest was heaving, and the material of my polo neck top was sodden by the time he pulled back. His eyes were red-rimmed and swollen. He sniffed and hiccupped twice before he gave me a watery smile. "I'm sorry." I arched my brow at him, and he chuckled wetly. "Touché. Okay, thank you for letting me cry all over you."

I cupped his cheeks and met his puffy eyes. "If you've been dealing with that crap all your life, then I'd say a couple of minutes crying is more than long overdue." I leant forward and kissed his soft lips. "He's a fool not to see what an amazing man you are."

He sighed and his breath mingled with mine. "All he sees is that I'm gay. An affront to him and the empire he's built for his one and only *gay* son."

My heart rate skipped a beat at what Maxim had spoken about in the hall. "Will you struggle without the trust fund?" I'd no clue what psychologists made. "I've a little money saved—"

"God you're so precious, but no, thank you." Brett laid his forehead against mine. "I've never used the trust fund, not since I got my doctorate.

Father would know that if he bothered to check." Brett chuckled, and his eyes gleamed with a hidden knowledge that set my heart racing.

"You did something, didn't you?" I asked as he stepped back, causing me to drop my hands.

"You could say that," he answered noncommittally.

I let it drop and checked the time. "What are you going to do about the party tonight? Maxim is bound to be there." I'd already made my mind up that whatever Brett wanted, I'd go with it.

"I was looking forward to you getting all dressed up and taking me dancing. I say let's go, and stuff what father thinks."

His face flushed with colour, and I stayed where I was with great difficulty, when all I wanted to do was kiss him for his bravery. I'd spent three days teasing us both, and I knew if I touched him right then, we'd never leave the room. "I'll go back to my room then and get dressed with that in mind." With a saucy wink, I walked to the door, then turned to look him dead in the eye. "Leave off your underwear. I'll want easy access later." His indrawn breath was the last thing I heard as I exited his room.

Hopefully that would give him something to distract from Maxim's crappy behaviour while he got ready. As I headed to my room, I was already mentally sorting through all the things I brought with me.

A fraught hour later, I stood in front of the mirror and eyed my outfit critically. The subtle foundation I'd used gave me a flawless complexion without looking heavy or caked on, but my eyes were a daring splash of colour in reds and purples, to match the deep plum of my lips and nails. Thankfully, in my haste to get ready, I'd managed not to smudge them. The handmade necklace created for me by a dear friend, matched the deep purple corset vest I'd had Charlie make for me. The plum-and-black satin alternated in panels of solid colour and those of an intricate woven damask design. The bone supports and the laces up the centre of my back help to sculpt my figure and cinch in my waist, making it appear tiny. I'd chosen a simple, black fitted shirt, which I'd left open to the V of the corset so you could see the necklace, and a pair of slim-fit black trousers that hugged me perfectly. Lastly, the whole outfit was finished off with a pair of suede, thigh-high stiletto boots, also in plum, to match the corset. The criss-cross of black laces that travelled up the outer edge of each boot, and the eight-inch heel, gave the impression

I had legs for days! The overall effect was classic, but sexy, and after recalling how Brett had looked at me the first time he'd seen me in boots, I was hoping I'd keep him distracted all night.

The dark purple jockstrap I'd slipped on before I'd dressed was a nice little New Year surprise for Brett. My body started to take notice of where my head was going and I worked to think about something else as my trousers, which were already tight, became tighter still. There was no way I'd be able to conceal my arousal. I eyed my trousers and shook my head. Fuck it!

I grabbed my large black fan, opting to go jacketless as we'd be staying in the hotel and it was already quite warm. Seconds later, I was out the door with my credit card tucked into my corset, congratulating myself on managing to be ready in such a short timeframe. I pulled up short when I came face to face with Maxim. I should have realised he wasn't the type to let things be.

He didn't mask the disgust in his face after his gaze swept me from head to toe. I cocked out my hip and flicked my fan. The snap brought his gaze to meet mine, and I was thankful for the height my heels gave me. "Is there something you want?"

His eyes narrowed on me. "I want you to leave my son alone." His Russian accent was harsh as his nostrils flared.

I'd had experience with bullies in the past, and though my stomach quivered, I met his angry stare. "I'm sorry, I can't do that. If Brett isn't interested in pursuing more with me then it will be his choice, *not yours.*"

"He's only showing interest in you to annoy me," he spat at me with venom.

"If that were the case, then you wouldn't be here now, asking me to keep away from him." I took a step closer, showing him I wasn't going to be intimidated as my hand tightened on my fan.

"I have feelings for your son. The kind that are serious. You can accept it and be part of Brett's life or go take a long jump off a short pier. I'll hope you'll opt for option one because your son loves you and I want him happy. Something you should want for him too." As Maxim's mouth opened, I snapped my fan closed and pointed it at him. "I've heard enough of your bullshit. Own your shit. He's gay, nothing you're going to do or say changes that."

A vein in Maxim's temple throbbed as he reached out and grabbed my arm, his face darkening by the second. My heart thudded erratically, but I was proud of myself for not flinching, determined not to let this man see my fear.

"If you think-"

Without allowing him the chance to finish his sentence, I brought the wooden handle of my fan down across his knuckles, causing him to wince and let go.

"Get your hand off me," I snapped, once again pointing my fan at him. "I have spent a long time putting this outfit together, so that I will look positively fabulous for *your son*. If you think I'm going to let the grubby little meat-paws of a pathetic man like you ruin the effect, you've got another think coming. And if you *ever* lay a hand on me again, I will do things to you with this fan that would make even the most depraved porn stars blush. Am I understood?"

The crack of my fan reverberated around the corridor like a gunshot as I snapped it open, my mask of fury leaving me cold as I took a step back and sidestepped Maxim, praying he wouldn't follow me as I walked to Brett's room.

Halfway there, Maxim called out, "You'll not feel like that when he's no access to his trust fund." I spun around on my heel, barely keeping control when the thin stiletto dug into the carpet, nearly ruining the effect.

I gave him a head-to-toe look, much like he'd done to me, before I sneered, "If you truly believe that all your son is worth is the money in his account, then you're a sadder individual than I thought." With that, I carefully swung back around to come face to face with Nanna.

She gave me a smile that belied the temper sparking in her eyes, then patted my arm. "Well said."

She looked past me to Maxim and pinned him with a lethal glare. "A word, Maxim." She gave my arm one more squeeze before she walked towards Maxim.

A part of me wanted to witness what was going to happen, but the other part, the part that knew Brett might come to get me, got me heading on down the hall. As I got to Brett's door, I glanced down the hallway to see Nanna guiding Maxim away. I released a shaky breath as I knocked on Brett's door and hoped that tonight wasn't going to be a disaster.

CHAPTER NINE

Brett

Air hissed past my teeth, and I wasn't sure if I were going to be able to hide my body's reaction to the sight of Guy, as he stood there looking utterly breath-taking.

He cocked out his hip, one hand on it as he gave me a sinfully sexy smile. "You ready to party?"

The smooth voice caressed a certain part of me as I watched Guy lick at his dark plum lips. An image of what my cock would look like with that purple smeared over it popped into my head and made it impossible to keep control of my libido. I shifted, and Guy's eyes twinkled as they lowered.

"You're...looking a little snug there." His wicked laugh didn't help as he stepped into my space and his lips brushed against mine. "I promise to take care of that...later."

I moaned in delight as his mouth pressed firmly against mine, and I tasted plum as his tongue teased my lips and I opened to him. The heels he wore forced me to tilt my head back a little, and for the first time in my life, I felt small and delicate as his mouth claimed me.

The surge of arousal was brutal, as was how overpowered he made me feel. The need to be in control slipped away, and for longer than I could remember, I accepted how it made me feel. Although Guy was that much younger than me, and probably lacked the experience I had, it didn't show as he took charge, and I went pliant against him. Why had I always needed to be in control? I chose not to point out the obvious and simply let myself be guided by Guy.

Breathless and harder than rock, Guy finally released my mouth and offered me a smile that should be outlawed.

"If we carry on, my trousers might split." Guy glanced down and drew my gaze.

"Oh fuck," I breathed, seeing the cock pressed obscenely against the zip of his trousers. My hands balled at my sides, my fingernails digging into my palms to resist reaching out to touch.

"Yes, that." He chuckled and closed his eyes as he took several deep breaths before looking at me again. "Maybe I need to go back and get a jacket, because the scent you're wearing, and that suit, are both doing a number on me. Never mind the sweet taste of your mouth, or the fact I know you're commando under those trousers." He gave a dramatic sigh that didn't hurt my ego one bit.

It was my turn to chuckle. "Then we're both in the same boat because, fuck me senseless, look at you."

He carefully stepped back, allowing me a better view as he snapped open his fan, causing my smile to widen at the message written in bold pink; *not today, Satan'*. "Right, my sweet man, let's go show these people how to party."

Paloma Faith sang about how life couldn't get better than this, and I'd say that right then, it couldn't. As the time ticked closer to midnight, I swayed tipsily on the dance floor with Guy. The hotel's large ballroom had been decorated for the evening in a hell of a lot of silver. Everywhere I looked it glittered, along with all the people who'd made the effort to join the party.

The room was packed with men and women who were all enjoying the flowing champagne and delicious food that kept appearing on the tables throughout the night. It was by far one of the best

New Year parties I'd ever been too, and it was all because of Guy.

A ball of emotion lodged in my throat from how special I felt in Guy's company. He treated me like I was a precious gift and the most important person in the room. It was a little overwhelming, especially when he'd spent the majority of the night making sure everyone there knew we were together.

I'd opted earlier not to search the room for Father, having decided to sit at a table with Griffin, Charlie, and Agnes. Griffin hadn't given Guy's outfit a second glance, but Nanna had been more than a little vocal about how fabulous he looked, and she wasn't wrong. I was proud to be the one on his arm. Whether it was because I was with Guy or not, Father had kept his distance, even when Mother came to say hello and stopped to chat with Agnes for several minutes.

After Mother had left, Agnes and Guy had gone off to a quiet corner, making me wonder what they were up to as they talked for over half an hour. Whatever it was, it had put a smile on Guy's face. I let it go when neither seemed inclined to talk about it when they returned.

Guy's arms tightened around my waist and his mouth went to my ear. "Are you having a good time?"

A shiver raced down my spine as his hot breath touched my skin. With his body pressed against mine, I was sure he could feel my arousal. I moved my head back a little so I could look at him. "This is, by far, the best New Year's Eve party I've ever been to."

Although the music was loud, I was sure he'd heard me as his smile deepened and he got a devilish light in his eyes. "Oh, is that so? And we haven't even got to the fun part of the evening yet." His lips, still deep plum, brushed against mine as he mouthed, "Have you ever been fucked in front of a mirror by a man in heels?"

The air got trapped in my chest and my arse clenched at the vivid imagery my mind conjured up. I'd not let anyone top me in nearly twenty years. Was I ready to let Guy?

With no time to answer, someone started the countdown to the New Year and Guy held my gaze, his blue-grey eyes full of emotions. Then, as midnight struck, his mouth captured mine and the world around us ceased to exist. All the emotion I'd seen in his eyes was in the kiss and it captured my heart in that moment. It was soft and sweet as his mouth worked to convey his feelings in a kiss that stole my breath.

It went on and on as people cheered and shouted around us, but I didn't pay them any attention. My sole focus was the man burrowing himself inside my heart.

"You are a true gift for New Year," he whispered against my mouth before he lifted his head to tilt it towards the exit. "Do you want to leave?"

There was a clear invitation in his eyes and my heart thudded erratically against my ribs, causing my hands to shake as I nodded. My mouth was too dry to talk.

As he led me towards the door, I caught sight of my father. From where he was stood, he'd have had a clear view of the kiss Guy and I had exchanged. He was too far away for me to read his expression in the dimly lit room, but his stiff posture was not. I swallowed a sigh and looked away. *Don't let him spoil your evening!*

I kept that on repeat as Guy led me to the bank of lifts to take us up to his room. The number of people stood at the lift meant Guy could do no more than hold my hand, but his eyes were full of promise.

A buzz from the alcohol combined with my pulse caused a fluttery feeling deep inside me as we exited the lift and walked hand in hand to Guy's room. The second the door shut behind him, he spun me around and his mouth was on mine. Alcohol and the taste of his lipstick flooded my mouth as he devoured me.

His hands appeared to be everywhere as he moved me until my back was pressed up against the door he'd just shut. "Do you know how *hard* it's been to keep my hands off you?" As if to prove the point, he started to tug off my suit jacket, tie, and shirt. Seconds later, I was naked from the waist up. He didn't give me any time to feel self-conscious over my pot belly, groaning when his hooded gaze roamed down my naked torso. His hands skimmed over my chest, pinching my budded nipples and causing me to cry out, my eyes slamming shut as he chuckled.

"So beautiful." His mouth was back on mine as his fingers played for a few more seconds before they roamed lower, towards my belt.

A groan of pleasure filled my mouth as Guy's hands skimmed over my stomach. "Your skin is soft, like silk. I can't wait to feel it against mine," he whispered.

A breathless moan left my parted lips before he claimed them again. Kiss after kiss, he drugged me with the passion he felt. It left me lost in a sea of pleasure that made it impossible to think about what he wanted to do to me.

By the time he was kneeling in front of me, with my trousers by my ankles and my cock down his throat as he stared at me with desire, I'd have done anything he wanted. The sound of slurping was drowned out by my moans and whimpers as he took me to the edge. His mouth was a warm heaven I never wanted to leave.

On the brink, my body flooded with a tingling sensation that lodged itself in my balls as Guy swallowed and his throat clasped the head of my cock. "Arghhhh fuckkk," I wailed, only for Guy to quickly pull off. I panted and gasped, my eyes begging him to continue. "Why'd...you...stop?"

His eyes twinkled. "Because I want to be buried deep in your arse when you come." He tapped my leg. "Lift up, let's get you naked."

I did as he indicated as a wave of embarrassment flooded my face when I realised how close he was to my stomach, now he wasn't trying to suck my brains through my cock. Glancing anywhere but at him, my cock flagged, and Guy hesitated as I lifted my other leg for him to take off my shoe and trousers.

"What's wrong?" His voice was soft as he stroked my leg. "Look at me, Brett."

I sighed and did as he asked, the feeling of acute mortification increasing when I attempted to suck in my belly. This appeared to do nothing more than draw Guy's attention to the area I didn't want him looking at.

I remained silent, unable to voice how inadequate I felt right then, naked and vulnerable in the harsh lights. He kept his gaze locked with mine as he finished removing my clothes and then got up off his knees.

His gaze swept over my body in a heated stare that seemed to scorch me as he towered over me in his heels. His hand dropped to his own cock, drawing my attention. "Do you see how aroused I am?"

Chewing on my lower lip, I nodded, keeping my gaze on the hand that continued to stroke the hard cock beneath his black trousers.

"You did this to me. The taste of you. The feel of you. The scent of you. You're beautiful and intoxicating. Do you remember what I promised you?"

Fear of rejection faded away as I swallowed hard. The image he'd created earlier returned as he glanced at the wall-length mirror that was situated by the wardrobes. Again, I couldn't find the words, so I nodded once more as my cock plumped at thoughts of what was to come.

His eyes lit with fire as he gave me a salacious grin. "I always keep my promises. Now go and grab the chair over there by the side of the bed and place it in front of the mirror."

My cock bobbed as I walked to the chair in question, trying not to look at the large bed where I'd be less exposed.

CHAPTER TEN

Guy

Brett's jerky movements as he went to retrieve the chair and the way he eyed the bed longingly gave me a moment's hesitation. Then I recalled how he'd got lost in the moment, not in the least bit bothered about his body when I'd been pleasuring him.

With that in mind, I went to my bag to get supplies, not wanting to have to stop later to get them. I swayed my hips sexily as I walked back to Brett. There was desire mixed with apprehension in his eyes, but I hoped that by the time I'd finished, all there would be was desire.

I placed the lube and condom on the chair he'd positioned in front of the mirror with the seat facing forward. As the back wasn't solid it would give Brett a view of my boots as I made love to his scrumptious arse.

Standing to my full height, I slowly undid the corset fastenings at the front, letting it drop to the floor before I opened my shirt and discarded it. Although I was slimmer than Brett, I was by no means sculpted, but his pupils dilated at the sight of my milky white skin and pink budded nipples. My chest was hairless, as was the rest of me because I waxed. I loved the little blond happy trail Brett had and the trimmed hair at the base of his cock, which was firming by the second.

As I ran my hand over my chest and down to the button on my trousers, I debated for a couple of seconds about removing my boots to take off my trousers. Deciding against it, I tugged my zipper down to reveal my jockstrap before I pulled out my cock and stroked it. The head gleamed in the overhead light while Brett licked his lips.

"I bet those pretty lips would look amazing wrapped around my cock, but right now, all I want is to sink inside you," I rasped as he trembled, his hand mimicking mine as he stroked himself in time with me. The touch was too much, yet not nearly enough as I watched his eyelids lower and his lips part as he pleasured himself.

"So beautiful," I murmured as I strode to him. "But I think you'll look even better bent over the chair, watching me claim your arse."

He shuddered and moaned. The slit of his cock pearled with drops of pre-cum before they dripped onto the carpeted floor.

"You want that, don't you? You want me to make you mine?"

"Oh, fuck...yes," he gritted out through clenched teeth, a look of desperation on his face as he started to thrust his hips and increase his strokes.

I sucked in a shaky breath as my balls tightened at the sight he made. "Bend over the chair, let me look at you." He didn't hesitate as he presented his delectable arse to me, his hooded gaze meeting mine in the mirror.

The excitement in his eyes added to my own as I stroked my hand down his flank. I praised him as I continued to hold his gaze, leaning around him to grab the condom. Once gloved, I reached for the lube and made a show of coating my fingers while pressing my cock against his bare buttock.

His chest heaved as I moved one hand to his cock while I slid my fingers down the crease of his arse to his warm hole. He groaned and pressed back as I used my fingertips to coat his tight rim. "Does that feel good?"

"Yes, so good...I've forgotten how good," he answered breathlessly, pleasing me with his reply.

As I breached him with the tip of my finger, I crowded over him, keeping my eyes on him. "Bear down," I said, brushing a kiss over his ear as he did as I asked, groaning with him as his tight channel clasped my finger.

"Fuck, you're so tight. I can't wait to feel you grip my cock. Can you imagine how good that's going to feel?" As I spoke, I slowly fingered his arse while feeling for his prostate.

A low growl and hip buck told me I'd found it, so I focused my attention there until he was mewling and moving his bottom hard and fast against me. I slipped in a second finger and he cried out, but before I could question if I'd hurt him, he was thrusting harder, while tunnelling his cock through my fingers.

"Oh gods, yes. This, fuck me. Harder, fuck," he begged and pleaded as his frantic gaze remained on me.

"Oh, sweets, I plan to," I gritted out through my clenched jaw, the passion on his face too much for me to deny him. I worked quickly to stretch him, so he'd be able to take me.

"Enough, I'm ready, pleaseeeee." He bowed back, trying to impale himself on my fingers, nearly causing me to stagger backwards.

My heels, thankfully, were dug into the carpet so I could brace. "Such an impatient sweet boy."

I licked my lips as I released his cock to take hold of his hips and keep him still while I shifted and slid the head of my all-too-sensitive cock against his slick hole. The heat penetrated the condom and burned me. Sweat gathered on my brow as I carefully pushed in past the rim of tight muscle, keeping my eyes on Brett's in the mirror.

He groaned long and low, but he didn't move as I sunk in, inch by inch. The tight clasp was better than I'd imagined as the muscle worked to crush my dick. I panted as I struggled not to come the minute my groin connected with his backside.

"Fuck, you're so tight."

"Shut up...or I'll...come before you move."

His pulsing channel spoke to his struggle and tempted me. I slowly withdrew, keeping my eyes on his. "Oh? But what fun would that be. Your arse is a thing of beauty, and I'm going to come all over it then lick it all off before I kiss you."

A shudder ran through him as he jerked, his eyes turning wild right as I thrust hard and fast back into him.

"Please, more," he cried out with a grunt, his hands reaching for the base of the chair for more purchase as he pushed back.

"Oh sweets, I'll give you anything you want." With that, all that could be heard was the slap of skin against skin and our combined grunts and moans. My legs weakened when his mouth opened and he continued to hold my gaze as cum jettisoned through the gap in the back of the chair, all over the base, with some splashes hitting the mirror.

His whole body convulsed as his arse tightened painfully around my cock and I struggled to not come in his arse. With as much care as I could muster, I withdrew my cock, even though it was the last thing I wanted right then, but I'd promised to coat his arse and lick it off.

I removed the condom with trembling fingers and followed him over the edge into orgasmic bliss after two strokes to my cock. My hips faltered and my legs shook while my balls emptied spurt after spurt of cum over his pale arse. It glistened in the light as he moaned.

On shaky legs, I stepped back and knelt to lap up the cum coating his skin. When I'd finished, I tugged at him until he ended up on the floor next to me. I twisted my upper body so I could face him.

His nostrils flared as his dazed expression met mine and I lowered my mouth to his to share my bounty. It was hot and dirty, but he didn't stop kissing me until he'd licked all of my mouth.

Breathless and weak at the knees, I laid my forehead against his. "This is the best New Year I've ever had, thank you, Brett. Happy New Year."

His eyes glimmered and he sucked in a shuddery breath. "Same…Happy New Year," he whispered.

The flavour of my cum coating his breath mingled with mine as I kissed him harder, not wanting the night to end—ever.

CHAPTER ELEVEN

Brett

Mother had remained silent as my father got into the back seat of the limo, giving me a look I'd not been able to interpret as he'd sat opposite me. That had been two hours ago, and the atmosphere in the car had become unbearable as we travelled back to Zurich.

The fun I'd had with Guy seemed like a lifetime ago, even though I'd only left him three hours prior. We'd been inseparable since New Year's Eve, staying hidden in his suite throughout the last two days as he'd done all manner of things to me over every piece of furniture the suite held. It would seem being with a man fifteen years my junior brought out all manner of things in me.

Heat spread up past the collar of my shirt, and I kept my gaze firmly on the passing scenery. The stirring in my pants was not what I wanted right then, so I shifted, causing my backside to throb. Guy had done what the men I'd dated had failed to do—lay claim to my arse. It was his, and he'd made sure I'd known it by the time I needed to pack my bags.

Only problem was, it wasn't the only thing he'd laid claim to. He'd claimed my heart too. It wasn't just the sex either, although he was a generous lover, and though he was a bossy top, he made me feel special and sexy. Something I'd not felt in a long time. With only the scenery to occupy me for the last couple of hours and a little breathing space to remove the cloud of lust, I could see he was the whole package. He was kind, generous, attentive, and most all, he wasn't afraid to stand up for me against the one person I'd struggled to deal with, my father.

The offer of money, now I'd had time to think about it and knowing more about his past, showed just how generous he was. Who freely offered what they had like that for someone that, at the time, they hardly knew? Money must be tight, and yet he'd offered his to me. What must it have been like to be brought up by a single parent, who'd worked two jobs to ensure their child could have their lifelong dream?

I eyed the man opposite me, whose head was buried in the file he held. Had he ever asked me what I wanted? As I searched my memory and came up blank, my mood darkened. Why couldn't he just love me?

As if he felt my gaze on him, Father's head lifted, and his unfathomable gaze met mine. His chest heaved, and for a moment, I thought he was going to say something, but then he looked down again and I sagged against the seat. My mother reached out silently and took hold of my hand, giving it a squeeze. There was understanding and frustration on her face as she looked between us.

It had always been the same. Mother accepted me, but she was trapped between me and my father, and as she loved us both, it was an untenable situation. It had taken years of training to gain my doctorate to give me that insight. And though as a child I'd wanted her to stand up to him, as an adult I got how hard that was.

"Are you going to be seeing that nice young man when you get back to London?" Mother asked, as if trying to break the tension in the car.

The whitening of the hand holding the file was the only sign my father had heard the question.

Twisting on the seat, I gave my mother my full attention as I smiled. "Yes. He's not flying back to London until Wednesday. However, he and Charlie have a lot to do to get ready for their fashion show for their finals."

"I heard Guy tell Agnes that Charlie made the corset he wore the other night, but that he'd designed it. He was kind enough to show me some of the sketches he's been working on. He's truly talented, the designs are stunning."

Out of the corner of my eye, I caught my father's brow arch almost as if in surprise. I nodded at mother. "He really is very talented, and he wants to make clothes for those who suffer with body consciousness issues." That was something he and I had talked quite a bit about after he'd pointed out several times that I needed to stop overthinking how I looked.

By the time I'd finished talking about Guy's vision, my Father had stopped pretending to read the file he held and was actively staring at both me and my mother.

Mother gave him a smile I was all too familiar with, one that said talk to me. I waited for the normal rejection.

"Does he have a sponsor for the show?"

My mouth dropped open, then snapped shut when he scowled at me.

"I've no idea. We didn't talk about money other than when he offered what little he had after you threatened to cut me off from my trust fund." As I recalled the threat, the sting

114

of hurt surfaced, even with the memory of Guy's generous offer.

My mother made a noise that was more suited to Agnes as she turned her full attention to my father. Her eyes narrowed in a look she didn't often use, and I held my breath, silently cursing for speaking my thoughts aloud. "Why did you do that? The whole reason for inviting Brett for these few days was for you to try and bridge the distance between the pair of you."

There was ice in her voice that said she knew the answer, but I was too focused on keeping my head from exploding. Was that really why he'd wanted me there, so he could make amends? Had it really had nothing to do with Blake Masters? I eyed my father when he eventually answered my mother, unsure how to take this new turn of events.

"We had a disagreement over him publicly touching his friend."

"You make it sound like I was touching his dick or something," I growled, causing mother to exhale sharply at my crude reply. I glanced at her. "I'm sorry, but enough is enough."

I shifted my gaze back to my father, recalling how Guy had stood up for me. "I have deep feelings for Guy. They aren't going to change just because you don't want me to be gay. I'm a gay man, get over it. I've spent years trying to please you, but I can't change something that is a

115

fundamental part of who I am." I sucked in the sob that got caught in my throat.

"Why can't you just love me for who I am?" I all but whispered into the silent car. It was the first time I'd had the courage to ask it aloud, and my ears thumped noisily with blood as I waited for him to answer.

My mother wrapped her arm around my shoulder, staying silent. It was then I realised I was shaking. My vision blurred as tears coursed down my cheeks. I was nearly forty years old, and still my father had the power to render me back to the teenage boy who just wanted his father to love him.

"I'm sorry. I...the life I came from...they'd kill a boy for being this way. I didn't want that for my son. The fear, it never leaves me." His voice was strained, and for the first time, he sounded genuinely concerned for me. I recalled all the times he'd refused to take me to Russia with him. Had he been worried for my safety?

"Then why didn't you tell me that?" I sobbed.

He dropped the file on the seat beside him, and before I could fathom what he was going to do, he moved to crouch in front of me and took hold of my hands. "I was brought up differently to many. My father wasn't progressive, and I was raised with hate and bigotry. It's hard to change some teachings, especially when all they gave me was fear of what would happen if my family found out what you were."

It didn't take a rocket scientist to figure what he meant as I tried not to take offence at what he was explaining.

"I've always loved you, son," he confessed. The truth behind his words was confirmed by the expression of fear he wore. He gave a wry chuckle as he looked at my mother then back at me. "It's hard to break the habits of a lifetime, but Agnes was only too happy to help me with my first lesson."

My brows arched as my mother burst out laughing, then my father joined in. The sound was so shocking, for a moment I couldn't quite believe my ears. Was my father laughing? What planet had I been transported to? But maybe, more to the point, what on earth had prompted Agnes to say something?

As if he'd read my thoughts, my father gave me a smile he had not aimed at me since I was a small boy. "Your boyfriend decided to give me a dressing down. Agnes overheard us and decided I needed a lecture on how to be a proper father."

The thickness of his accent this time wasn't because of anger, and I didn't know what to do, having never seen this softer side of my father in decades. A part of me was half-expecting someone to jump out and tell me I'd been pranked. But as he continued to hold my hands, it hit that this was really happening, that he did indeed love me. With the years of craving this moment, I worked to push the old hurt aside and focus on the here and now.

I encouraged my mother to move along the seat and make room next to me for my father to sit. When he did, I did something I'd not done in some thirty plus years, I rested my head on his broad shoulder.

He stiffened fractionally before he moved to tug me closer and whispered, "*мой мальчик я люблю тебя*."

My eyes burned as I buried my face into his scented neck as I quickly translated what he'd said, 'my boy, I love you'. "*Я люблю тебя, папа*," I replied, letting him know I loved him too.

CHAPTER TWELVE

Guy

C harlie grabbed the last of the bags of clothing off my bed. "Is this the last of it?" He glanced about the room as if I might have another bag hiding somewhere.

"Yep, though there are all the clothes I have stored," I added, tongue in cheek, knowing fine well most of the stuff was now in the back of the van we'd hired.

Since our return to uni, things had been full on, so much so we'd had little time to start on creating the clothing ready for our planned fashion show. So Charlie had suggested I move out of the uni digs and into one of the spare rooms in his home so we could work on the finals project in the evenings. I'd jumped at the chance; his house was by the beach and beautiful. The bedroom I'd bunked in on occasion when I'd gone out for a few drinks with him was huge compared to my current, cramped room.

"I'm not sure we'll get anything else in the van." Charlie's brows furrowed as he gave me a worried look.

"I'm joking. It's mostly in the van. I don't have that many clothes." His head tilted to the side as one brow arched up. "All right, I do have quite a few. But that's your fault, buying all those cast-off fashion pieces has only increased my fashion obsession."

"Yeah, yeah, blame me because you're a fashion whore." He chuckled, then rolled his eyes as I bowed at him.

"You forgot to add, 'sexiest' clothes whore."

Charlie's smile widened and his eyes got speculative. "Is that what Brett tells you?"

A wave of heat flooded my cheeks. "He might," I sighed mournfully, "if we ever got to see each other." I'd spoken to him every day since I'd got back to Brighton, but in the three weeks since my return, we'd not managed to arrange a date that suited us both. A smile formed on my face, remembering that was going to change this weekend. Brett was coming to Brighton tonight.

I eyed Charlie as my stomach jittered. "Do you think Griffin will mind if I have a guest stay in my room with me?" I held my breath, hoping I'd not need to find money to pay for a hotel. I'd got a bit carried away with purchasing fabrics on my return from Switzerland, with all the new ideas I'd had. I'd also bought extra material for Charlie to make a handmade waistcoat I'd designed for Brett, in the hopes of improving his self-image.

"—he can't hear them." Charlie stopped talking and looked expectantly at me.

Crap, having missed most of what he'd said, I gave him a sheepish smile. "Say again."

"I said, Griffin doesn't have a problem with guests as long as he can't hear them."

"Cool, I'm sure I can find a way to muffle Brett's screams of pleasure."

Charlie held up a hand and waved it at me. "Stop right there, I don't need to hear about what Brett does to you."

"That would be the other way around," I answered, causing Charlie's arm to drop at his side.

His eyes narrowed. "Really? I always thought you were a bottom, or at least a switch."

I shrugged, knowing that I had a tendency to present myself in a way that caused others to wrongly assume my preferences. Charlie knew me, but as we'd never got beyond a drunken kiss, he'd never seen my assertive side because it was something I kept to the bedroom. "I much prefer to top, and though I have switched, it doesn't do a whole lot for me."

The tap at the open door drew my attention to Chelci, who stood in the doorway holding a large, oversized bag, with a suitcase at her feet.

"Am I too early?" she asked as she glanced around the room, her pretty face full of excitement.

"Nah, perfect timing as always. I've stripped the bed and cleaned the room, so you can move straight in," I said, grinning at her. Chelci was a fashion major and in several of my classes. We'd worked together on projects and she was a fun girl to hang with.

When she'd heard I was moving out, she'd practically jumped me to get first dibs on the room because her roommate, who'd she'd been dating, had dumped her for someone else and seemed to take great pleasure in rubbing Chelci's nose in the new relationship.

"You're a sweetie, thank you for saving me from the ex." Her smile dimmed before she stepped into the room.

As she passed, I touched her arm. "There's someone amazing out there for you, you'll see."

"Thanks..." she trailed off as her eyes sheened, then she sucked in a tremulous breath, "but I'm sticking to being single for now. It's much less hassle and I've finals to focus on. I'm way behind because of she-who-shall-remain-nameless."

"If you need any help, just ask." I gave her arm another squeeze as Charlie spoke.

"Same goes, but, Guy, we need to get a shifty on if you want to get all the stuff in the van into the house sometime this year."

I stuck my tongue out at Charlie, making Chelci grin. "Alright, I'm coming."

In a flurry of activity, we put the rest of the bags in the overfull van after waving goodbye to Chelci. Charlie made good time to his home; the dark streets nearly empty at this time of the evening.

As we pulled into the drive, the security light lit up the front of the house, then the front door opened to reveal Nanna with a woman I didn't recognise. "Who's that with Nanna?"

Charlie released a long, drawn-out sigh. "That is the new companion, Rachael. And boy, it's like they reassembled the mould that made Nanna and then added in some extra mischief." He sounded resigned as he parked in the drive, and I laughed.

"There is no way they could replicate Nanna."

He glanced at me with an expression that made my lips clamp together to stop from laughing. "You wanna bet!"

With that, he opened the door and jumped out, so I followed suit. The bitter wind tugged at my coat as I scented the sea.

"Oh, Guy, look at you, pretty as a picture. Come and meet Rachael, I've told her all about you." Nanna's eyes gleamed with humour as she patted Rachael's arm. As I glanced at her, she wore an identical humorous expression, and I got a slight sinking feeling in my stomach when the woman held her hand out to me.

"It's lovely to meet you. I can't wait to see what clothes you've got hidden in that van. Agnes told me all about what you wore at New Year." She tittered and a pink-hue coated her cheeks. "I've a penchant for men in heels, so sexy."

This time it was me that was blushing as she eyed me from head to toe in a way that caused me to consider stepping back.

"I told you," Charlie muttered under his breath, chuckling as he passed to go and open the back of the van.

At a loss for words, I gave her a smile and quickly walked to the back of the van where Charlie was, in the hope they'd both take the hint and leave us to it. But no, they had other ideas.

"Right, Rachael, you grab what you can carry. Then we can help Guy empty his bags and see all the pretty things he has."

"Nanna, you're not rooting in Guy's things. What have I told you about privacy and boundaries?" Charlie sounded like a parent telling off a naughty child.

"Don't be silly, Charlie boy, how is helping with the unpacking breaching a boundary?" Nanna glanced at Rachael. "Young people today."

My lips twitched at how she turned her nosiness into being helpful. As I pondered how I was going to get out of the predicament, considering what I'd stashed in some of the bags, my phone rang. As I reached into my jacket pocket, Nanna and Rachael moved to the van and I groaned under my breath.

Then a smile spread over my face when I saw Brett's name on the screen. I took a few steps away from the van. "Hey, sweetie, you better be ringing to tell me you're in Brighton."

Brett's laughter filled my ear. "Anyone would think you've missed me."

"I'm going to show you tonight just how much I've missed you," I answered in a low, sexy voice, keeping my eye on the two ladies pulling bags out of the back of the van.

"Promises, promises."

"No, it's a threat. I plan to make sure you can't sit down for a week without thinking about me."

He gave a throaty moan and warmth spread through me.

"You know, talking to me like that when I'm driving is likely to make me cause an accident," Brett accused in a breathless voice.

"Okay, I'll behave…for now. Where are you?"

"I'm just about to exit the A23, can you give me directions to where you are?"

"Hang on, I'll pass you to Charlie so he can give you the directions to get here." I'd already told Brett I was moving in with Charlie for the remaining time I'd left in uni, so this wasn't news to him. "Charlie, can you explain to Brett how to get here, please?" I handed the phone to him when he nodded distractedly, after dropping a bag to free up a hand.

Behind him, Nanna stopped on her way to the door and looked back at me. She wore an odd expression on her face that left my nerves thrumming. "Is Brett coming to see you?"

"Yeah, he's going to spend the weekend with me." In my excitement, it took a moment to register the look that passed between her and Rachael, and I got the distinct impression Nanna had explained how dreadful Maxim had been at New Year.

The conversation we'd had at the party, after I'd left her with Maxim, had been enlightening. By all accounts, she'd reamed him a new arsehole and left him with several choice words about how he should learn to treasure his son.

Brett had mentioned that Maxim and he had words in the car and that things had improved between them. I hoped that it continued because Brett seemed much happier whenever he spoke about Maxim.

"Oh, how wonderful, a house full of boys. Griff will be home for the weekend too." Nanna gave me a wide smile before she carried on walking to the open front door. About to turn to Charlie, I heard her say to Rachael, "We'll need to root out the good clothes to be ready to party with the boys this weekend."

I choked on my saliva as Charlie rolled his eyes, clearly not having missed what she'd said while he handed me my phone.

Two minutes later, phone tucked back in my jacket pocket, I eyed Charlie. "She doesn't think she's coming clubbing with us, does she?"

He gave a mournful sigh. "Yep, and I'm telling you now, if you can get her to change her mind, then you're a better man than either Griff or me."

My heart beat erratically against my ribs, and for the first time since Charlie suggested I move in for a few months, I wondered if I was about to regret my decision.

"That look you have on your face right now is the correct reaction. She's a terror! And now she has Rachael, god only knows what havoc she'll cause," Charlie stated fatalistically. "Come on, let's get inside before she opens up one of your bags of toys."

A wave of dizziness swept over me as I rushed to grab whatever bags were closest to me, then ran to the open door like I was in the hundred-metre sprint, with Charlie's laugher following me.

Bloody traitor!

CHAPTER THIRTEEN

Brett

How I'd been hoodwinked into taking Agnes and her new companion, Rachael, out to dinner with me and Guy, I'd no clue. Charlie had been more than a little encouraging that we should take them out when he realised no one had eaten, but then cried off joining us because he wanted to wait for Griffin to arrive home. He'd been away all week, and his plane tonight had been delayed due to icy fog at the airport.

All the promises about what Guy was going to do to me were now on hold, not that I minded when he was sat next to me, his warm hand stroking my thigh.

Riddle and Finns The Beach had been recommended by Charlie, and they'd managed to squeeze us in for dinner. The place was right on the beach and though it was dark outside, I could imagine it gave a lovely view from the window seats in spring and summer. The noise level was such that you had to raise your voice a little to be heard, but the place had a great atmosphere, and if the scents coming from the kitchen were anything to go by, the food would be delicious. I eyed the table to the left of us as the waiter arrived with two fish dishes, and my stomach growled.

"Brett, it's so lovely of you to offer to take us out to dinner," Agnes said as she picked up the menu and eyed it critically.

Seeing no point in stating she'd given me no option, I gave her a smile. "It's my pleasure. I also think I probably owe you more than a meal after...your little chat with my father."

Her cheeks pinked as she paid extra attention to the menu and not me. Her hand came up and she waved it in the air, barely missing knocking over her water glass. "It was nothing. We'll say no more about it."

Rachael gave Agnes a nudge to her ribs, and they exchanged a look I didn't try to interpret as Guy muttered to me, "these two are trouble."

Seeing she didn't want to talk about my father, I laughed and shook my head when both women acted innocent. "You could be right." I got no further when the waiter appeared at the side of the table to take our orders.

Once he'd gone, I intertwined my fingers with the hand on my leg and gave Guy a warm smile. I'd missed him, and although we'd had daily talks via FaceTime, it wasn't the same as being with him. He was so full of life it was contagious, and I'd found myself eager to start my day, knowing I'd be spending time with him.

We'd had the boyfriend conversation and it was official, we were exclusive. It was a great feeling, especially with him looking at me the way he was right then.

"Guy, be careful or you might set Brett on fire with those looks."

Agnes's comment had Guy grinning as he glanced in her direction. "That's the plan, Nanna, that way it will melt the clothes right off his body."

The water I'd chosen just then to take a sip of splattered the tablecloth as I coughed and choked. "Seriously?" My eyes watered as I put the glass back down, and Guy helpfully banged me on the back as both Agnes and Rachael laughed. I avoided looking at the couple of tables close to us as I mopped up the water.

Guy shrugged. "If you can't beat them, join them. That's my motto."

When I finally managed to stop coughing, I gave him a mock glare. "Maybe next time you might want to warn me so I don't decide to spray the table with water."

"What fun would that be?"

It was the first time I was aware of the age difference between us as he grinned at me, his expression unrepentant. But for the life of me, I couldn't find it in me to see it as an issue as I returned his grin. "You're as incorrigible as Agnes."

He didn't get a chance to answer as our starters and drinks arrived at the table. Everyone became silent as we tucked into the food.

Several minutes passed before Agnes spoke. "I didn't realise the octopus would be this chewy."

Before I could answer, she went to tug the piece of offending octopus out of her mouth, only it wasn't the only thing to come out. My eyes widened as I watched the top set of her false teeth sail through the air and land with a splash in the New England clam and bacon chowder I'd ordered. In slow motion, the chowder crested the bowl, slopping onto the table, right before the teeth floated next to a clam.

There was a loud snort from my left side as Rachael roared with laughter. A hush fell over the rest of the restaurant, and I was sure every set of eyes were on us as the teeth floated in my starter. I wasn't sure if I wanted to vomit or laugh at how macabre my delicious chowder now looked.

The hush abruptly stopped, quickly followed by laughter both loud and muffled. I gave a resigned sigh as I pushed the bowl towards Agnes. "I think I might have something you want back."

That got Guy rolling on the seat next to me as Agnes covered her mouth with her napkin while she picked up my spoon and lifted out the false teeth. My stomach heaved as she dropped the napkin, picked up the teeth, licked them, and gave me a toothless grin. "Tasty," she lisped.

It was too much, and laughter bubbled out as Guy leaned against me, continuing to laugh uncontrollably. It took several minutes for everyone to gain control, and though Agnes was looking a little flushed, she stood and gave a bow to the restaurant, declaring in a loud voice, "Slippery little suckers."

More laughter followed and that set the tone for the evening. By the time we returned to the house, which was in darkness, my sides ached, and I was more than a little tipsy.

Guy ushered me to the room I'd left my weekend bag in. He quickly shut and locked the door before placing a finger over my lips.

"We need to keep the noise down." He traced my lips with his fingertips before they moved down my chin and around to the back of my collar. A shiver of excitement raced down my body at the soft touch.

"And how do you propose we keep the noise down?" I gasped as his fingers moved to grip my hair in a possessive hold while he brought me closer to his mouth.

"I suggest we get naked, get on the big comfy bed, and..." his lips brushed against mine as he whispered, "I suck your cock and you suck mine."

My moan was muffled as he took my mouth in a hard kiss. Heat and arousal combined to coat my skin in sweat in record time. The coat I still wore felt heavy and cumbersome as Guy continued to show me with his mouth how much he'd missed me.

The kiss was endless and full of passion. He sucked my tongue into his mouth as he groaned, and I felt myself being manhandled towards where I thought the bed was. But I didn't complain, not when I was as desperate as him for more. To feel him naked, pressed against me, his cock in my mouth.

I wasn't sure how many minutes it took as we frantically stripped out of our clothes between kisses. All thoughts of being quiet had somehow gone out the window by the time we tumbled onto the bed, sweaty and panting.

Aroused to the point of pain, Guy didn't seem to be in a much better condition, his cock hard and leaking. He moved to position me flat on my back before he twisted around and swung his leg over me to straddle my face, presenting his slick looking cock to me.

"Suck me, sweet boy," he rasped, a second before his hot, wet tongue circled the head of my cock. He groaned and then lapped at my slit, his tongue tormenting me as his hand gripped the base of my dick.

He wiggled his cock in my face and the scent of his arousal filled my nose as I inhaled. I shifted a little so I could easily suck the slick head between my lips. My arms were trapped at my sides by Guy, and somehow that feeling of powerlessness ramped up my excitement. He didn't force his cock down my throat but kept his hips high, just feeding me the mushroom head between my lips. I used my tongue much like he was, mimicking every move he made. The growls and rumbles vibrating around my cock were like rocket fuel being added to my body's already fuelled system.

The more sound he made, the more I wanted. Only, I was struggling to focus as he parted my legs, letting his saliva drip down my balls and taint towards my arse. I clenched in anticipation. My chest heaved as his fingers massaged my balls, bathed my cock in long, wet strokes, then adding suction to the head as he pulled off.

A full-body shiver started at my toes and worked its way up me until it hit my head, lifting the tiny hairs at the nape of my neck. He gave another hard suck and my balls tightened as a tingling developed in my lower spine. It spread faster than pins and needles, leaving me breathless and mindless, knowing what was coming.

Guy thrust the head of his cock a little deeper in my mouth and I sucked him as hard as he was sucking me and then his finger breached my arse and it was all over, bar the shouting. I trembled and shuddered as he used my saliva to help his finger glide in until his knuckles hit my arse cheek. After he'd spent the two days in his hotel room in Switzerland making sure he knew what I liked, he knew just where to go and his finger strummed against my prostate as I cried out around his dick.

The instant the first spurt of cum left my cock, Guy followed me over the edge and my mouth flooded with cum. I worked not to swallow, knowing that Guy would come to kiss me when he'd finish sucking me dry.

Sweaty and struggling not to swallow, Guy's cock slipped free from my lips and a few seconds later, he shifted to face me. A devilish smile lit his eyes as his mouth, still full of my cum, pressed to mine. The taste of him mixed with my essence, and my cock gave a futile attempt to buck at how fucking sexy it was to taste us both on my tongue.

"That is so fucking hot," I gasped after he finally released my mouth. He had cum smeared on his chin and I'd bet I was the same.

"Snowballing rocks. I love that you're as dirty as me." His smile was sinful as he gave me one final kiss before he collapsed onto the bed next to me. Then he grabbed the cover and tucked me into his side. His lips brushed my head. "I missed you," he whispered.

"I missed you too." My heart swelled, and I tried to tamper down the growing feelings that were getting harder to ignore with each passing day that I got to know him a little better. What if Guy was only looking for a short-term thing?

Don't borrow trouble, you know better than that.

I shut my eyes and worked to focus on the present moment. Because in the end, that was all anyone was guaranteed, right?

CHAPTER FOURTEEN

Guy

The weekend had flown by far too quickly, and I struggled to act positive as I stood next to Brett's car early Monday morning. He'd had to get up at the crack of dawn so he could head back to London.

"When do you think you can get down again? Next weekend?" I asked, unable to hide my hope. We'd avoided talking about him leaving, and when he'd next be free, up until this point.

"I won't be able to come Friday, unless..." he chewed his lower lip between his teeth, something I noticed he did when he was thinking.

I didn't prompt him but waited, though I did fidget with the collar of his coat.

"If I shuffled my last client Friday evening, I could get here about ten. Is that too late?"

Although not often, Brett revealed his vulnerabilities and it endeared him more to me than the confident man he showed the world.

"I don't care what time you get here, as long as you *come*."

His eyes lit with a fire and I knew exactly where his head had gone. I tugged him a little closer to me and dropped my hand. He groaned as I touched his partially aroused cock through his trousers. "You'll have to hold whatever thought you just had until Friday. Hopefully, it will make you try *harder*," I tightened my hold before stroking down the fabric of his trousers, "to come earlier...on Friday."

He groaned, and his eyes closed as he pushed his lower body more firmly against my hand. I chuckled, gave him a brief kiss, then stepped back. It didn't hurt my ego to see stark desire and disappointment as he looked at me.

"I suppose I better hit the road if I don't want to be late for my first appointment." His words lacked any enthusiasm as I nodded and watched him get into the car.

Once he'd fastened his seatbelt, I leant in and stole one more hard kiss. "That will hopefully keep you going until Friday."

"Not a chance," he responded, and I laughed as I stepped back to close his car door. I waited until his car had disappeared before heading back into the warm house. Shivers ran over my skin as I headed back up to my bedroom, only now realising standing outside in a T-shirt in the middle of winter was not for the faint-hearted.

I glanced at the unmade bed, but instead of crawling back into it like I wanted to, I headed to the bathroom for a shower. If I wanted to take another weekend off with Brett, then I was going to need to pull my finger out.

As I stripped and waited for the water to warm, I counted off the number of outfits that needed to be ready for our final show. I sagged at the scary number and how long it took me to work on any one individual piece.

Charlie was the sewing genius. Me, I was not horrendous, but I was definitely slower than a snail. It took me four times longer than Charlie to create anything. I was the design expert, and Charlie was the sewing whizz, which is why we made such a good team. He had the flare to make a piece look amazing when he handstitched them.

Handsewn garments fetched a much higher price, and though that was appealing, it was giving someone a bespoke piece of clothing that gave them newfound confidence that really drove me.

So many people had body confidence issues, myself included when I was younger. But my mum had taught me that it wasn't what was on the outside that made the person special, it was what was inside. With that in mind, I'd considered how the external clothing could boost confidence. At uni, I'd learned about the psychology of fashion. Stick-thin models and airbrushed figures in magazines added to the whole misconception of what is perceived as perfection. There was no human alive that was perfect. Everyone had their insecurities, and the business Charlie and I were aiming to set up was geared to real people and making them feel self-assured in our clothes.

We'd been mocked by some of the models in the industry, especially when we'd chosen real people to do our catwalk show. Charlie, who was a little more involved in the modelling world, had more than one run-in about our concept. Although Charlie was a model, it wasn't his long-term career goal or even his first choice of job, he'd done it purely to fund his education. There were many in the industry that didn't get why he wasn't going to continue modelling after uni, when he could pick and choose some of the most lucrative jobs in the business.

The long-term goal had always been to set up a business in Brighton once we'd got our degrees. That hadn't changed, though I had worried when Charlie met Griffin whether he'd be side-tracked by his billionaire boyfriend.

The steam gathering in the room alerted me to how long I'd been stood thinking. I stepped into the hot shower and quickly washed the scent of sex off me, trying not to think about Brett and how much I was going to miss him. He was so easy to be with that I could imagine what life could be like living with him. *Stop right there!*

I released a loud groan and worked to think on all the things I needed to do.

By the time I got out of the shower and was dressed, there were sounds coming from the house to indicate I wasn't the only one up.

As I opened my bedroom door, Griffin appeared out of a door down the hall. He nodded, his face hard and unsmiling. As he looked like that most of the time, I didn't take offence. "Morning," I sing-songed, receiving a grunted response in reply.

Charlie appeared a second later behind Griffin. "Hey, you're up early."

I was known for sleeping in. I was anything but a morning person, unless of course I was sleeping next to Brett. Then I was definitely a morning person. "Brett had to leave early. His plan was to return to London last night, so we compromised, meaning I had to get up at the arse crack of dawn."

Griffin made another grunting noise as he passed me, his face flushing a dark red. It would seem Griffin was a bit of a prude when it came to others' naked adventures. He'd not been too happy, or so Charlie had said, on Saturday night after I'd fucked Brett up against the door, causing quite a bit of noise.

"Yes...we heard you compromising," Charlie winked at me as he strolled over the wooden flooring, "didn't we, Griff?"

"Fuck off," came the reply from Griffin as he went downstairs, not once looking back.

I chuckled. "He won't decide to throw me out will he," I asked in a low voice.

"He might," came the shout from the bottom of the stairs.

Charlie shook his head and shouted back, "No, he won't, not if he doesn't want to forget what his cock is for."

There was a loud curse, followed by feet thudding on wood and the sound of a door slamming.

I glanced at the staircase, then back at Charlie, who didn't seem the least bit bothered by Griffin's show of temper. "Ignore him. He's feeling a little frustrated as he has to go away again. He hates to leave me." Charlie shrugged, but his own face lost a little of the humour it had shown.

"It sucks, right?" I rubbed at his arm, thinking about how I'd felt, knowing I wouldn't get to see Brett till Friday.

"Yeah, it sucks, but I have you and Nanna to keep me occupied. All Griff has is work." Charlie sighed forlornly. "Come on, let's go get breakfast, then we can figure out which designs we should create first." He carried on talking as we went downstairs, along the hall and into the large open-plan kitchen. The view of the beach this morning was spectacular, and I stopped to look at the sun cresting the sky as it turned it into a glorious array of pinks and purples. The sea glittered as the wind picked up the water.

I'd never lived near the sea before moving to Brighton, and I'd found I had a love of the sea I'd not expected. The scent of the salty air was addictive, and I'd often, in the summer months, go and sit on the pier, eat fish and chips, and people watch. It was one of my favourites past times.

"Did you get all the measurements we needed for those we've picked to model for us," Charlie asked, drawing my attention from the large windows.

"Yep, I did. I'm hoping that it's not too soon. As we all know, the winter is when we get comfy with our food."

Charlie grinned. "Oh god, yes, there is nothing better in the winter than snuggling in front of the fire with a movie on the TV and a big bag of treats."

At that moment, Nanna walked into the kitchen from the door that led into the annex on the side of the house, Rachael right behind her.

"You, Charlie boy, love to do that all year round, so stop kidding yourself." She came to me and gave me a kiss on the cheek.

The scent of lilies surrounded me. This morning she wore a kind of lounge suit in bright orange. Her hair was silver and styled in a chic bob that made her appear much younger than her eighty-three years. "You're looking very bright and chipper this morning, Nanna."

She gave my arse cheek a pinch. "Not as bright and chipper as you I bet." I blushed and Charlie groaned.

"You asked for that," he pointed out to me, before he shook his head at Nanna. "You shouldn't be thinking about...well...you know." He stumbled over his words as Nanna arched her brows and gave him an innocent look, though it failed miserably as her eyes gleamed with mischief.

"You could be right. But as much as I'd love to talk about my sex life. I've a million pieces of clothing that need to be handstitched—"

"We can help," Nanna interrupted, then glanced back at Rachael who was stood listening with a wide smile on her face, "can't we, Rachael?"

"Can you sew?"

"Can I sew?" Nanna huffed and pointed at Charlie. "Who do you think taught Charlie boy?"

My eyes narrowed on her and Charlie stepped closer to Nanna. "We can't expect you to help—"

"Why not?" Nanna and I asked in unison.

We glanced at each other and laughed. "What she said."

Charlie gave me a look I knew all too well, one that said I was making a big mistake. But for the life of me, I couldn't see an issue. Sewing wasn't taxing, and if it meant we could get ahead of the game, then I was all for it.

"On your head be it," Charlie muttered as he stalked to the cupboard. Nanna gave me a triumphant smile and I felt a thread of unease. Had I just made a big mistake?

CHAPTER FIFTEEN

Brett

There was a part of me that had known the other shoe would drop eventually, after I'd made the decision to move the majority of the trust fund money. If I'd secretly hoped it would be never, who could blame me after things had started to improve with my father.

It was Thursday, and I could tell the day was going to turn to shit when my secretary had interrupted my session with a client. This was something I had drummed into her should never happen unless the world was about to explode. Clearly the world was not about to explode, but evidently my father was if he didn't get to speak to me.

Chloe, my secretary, was teary on the phone as she explained why she'd broken my rule. "I'm so sorry, but your father has rung nine times in the last forty-five minutes, and I know that your session with Will is for two hours, but he is refusing to listen to me when I say I can't interrupt you. I don't know what to do anymore. I've tried everything to placate him."

I knew all too well how much of a bully my father could be when he wanted something. Evidently, he wanted to talk, and it could only be about one thing if he was this insistent— money.

"Ask him to hold, I'll be out in a moment." I sucked in a shaky breath as I put my phone down and walked back around my desk.

I looked back at Will and my chest tightened. He was so frail, and the haunted look on his face seemed to increase as I silently cursed my father. "I'm so sorry, but there seems to be an emergency I need to deal with. It should only take a few minutes. I'll get Chloe to bring you a hot chocolate."

"It's okay," Will muttered as his hands clasped together and twisted nervously.

It had taken me months to get the abused young man to talk to me. It was why we had a double session because he tended to need an hour to relax enough to speak. I prayed this interruption wouldn't set us back.

Exiting my office, I shut the door softly behind me as I glanced at Chloe, giving her a reassuring smile. "Can you make Will a hot chocolate, please."

She nodded. "I'm so sorry, but I did try everything." Her eyes gleamed with unshed tears.

"Listen, I know what he's like. I'm the one who's sorry you've had to put up with his nonsense." I sighed and pointed to the small office that was empty. "Transfer his call to the spare office, please. I'll take it in there."

Resigned to what was coming, my stomach danced with nerves as I shut the door behind me in the slightly stale smelling room.

It took several deep breaths before I found the courage to lift the phone after it started to ring. "Hello, Father—"

"Why didn't you mention you've moved the money out of the trust fund? What have you done with it?" His tone was harsh and suspicious. I was transported back to my childhood, and I braced my hand on the desk as my legs shook.

"It's nice of you to ring me, but I'm with a client. As I've discussed before, it is imperative that you listen to my secretary when she tells you I'm busy. How would you feel if I barged in on one of your meetings? It's not acceptable. With regards to the money, that trust fund is mine to do with as I wish. I do not have the time or the patience to discuss this right now. If you are free this evening, I will come to the house so we can talk about my *money*."

There was a sharp inhale and a muttered curse in Russian. "Fine, I'll tell your Mother you'll be coming for dinner."

There was an odd quality to his voice that I couldn't explain as I finished the call and headed back to my office.

The afternoon seemed to fly by with the reality of what was going to happen later. As my last client left and the door shut behind them, I sagged into my leather seat. Right then, I wanted one thing, Guy. I craved to feel his arms around me and to hear him tell me how special I was.

With that thought in mind, I opened my office desk and pulled out my silenced mobile, opening the FaceTime app to dial Guy. Today was a short one for Guy, he'd only had classes this morning, so I hoped he was back at Charlie's and could talk for a few minutes. The second his smiling face appeared on the screen, a sob got caught in my throat.

"Who's upset you?" he demanded as he started to move, and the room behind him disappeared, along with the noise of several voices.

"I'm sorry. Am I interrupting you?" I hiccupped as I sucked back the next sob, not wanting to sound pathetic.

His brows drew together and his eyes narrowed as he peered at me. "Of course you're not interrupting me. I love when you call. But you're avoiding answering my question. Who upset you? Or should I take a random stab and say your father?" His bedroom appeared behind him, followed by the sound of a closing door.

"Not so random when you know what a dick he can be. And yes, he's upset me." I hesitated. Would mentioning the obscene amount of money I had change things between us?

Up to now, I'd avoided any mention of money. On the couple of occasions we'd been out, we'd taken turns to pay for things. Guy hadn't mentioned anything again about money after he'd offered what he had to me.

I rubbed at my temple, feeling the headache that had been brewing since I'd spoken to my father, gathering momentum.

"Talk to me, sweets." Guy's eyes grew concerned as the silence lengthened.

"Do you remember the conversation when my father threatened me over my trust fund?" He looked a little confused, but he nodded. "Before I went to Switzerland, I moved the majority of that trust fund to another account on the recommendation of my financial advisor." I licked my now dry lips and glanced at the glass of water on my desk.

I reached for it as Guy's head tilted to the side and he got a thoughtful look on his face as I took a deep drink.

"That solves your problem of him manipulating you, doesn't it?"

I placed the glass down with a shaking hand, then met his gaze. "It's not that simple. The account held a lot of money."

His eyes widened a fraction. "A lot of money, as in thousands?"

Heat rode up my neck and I struggled to hold his steady stare. "Erm a little more than that." I drew in a deep breath, then rushed to say, "two billion."

There was an odd gasping sound as Guy's face disappeared, and I realised he'd dropped his phone.

"Guy? Guy, are you still there?"

A second later, his face reappeared and he looked a little paler than before. Shit, had I just fucked things up?

"Did you say *two billion*?" he whispered, as if scared of my answer.

I nodded, my eyes begging him to...what? I'd no clue. I wasn't sure what kind of reaction I'd been expecting, but when he remained silent, with glassy eyes, my stomach twisted into painful knots.

"I think you might have undersold the whole 'a little more than thousands', sweets."

Somehow, the use of the term of endearment he tended to use in lieu of my name eased the tension inside me. I chuckled wryly, "Yeah, you could be right."

"I take it Maxim has just found out you've moved the money and is a little pissed."

I knew it wouldn't take Guy long to figure out what had happened. "A little pissed might be the understatement of the year. Especially when he finds out how much of it I've given away to charity."

Guy laughed, the rich sound making me feel better as it wrapped around me, much like his arms did when we slept together. "Oh, I wish I could be there to see his face when you tell him."

"I wish you could be here too. I'm going to dinner tonight at my parents, in"—I checked my wristwatch—"an hour's time."

His smile dimmed as his finger traced over the screen. "I've missed you." He sighed, and something passed between us that caused an ache in my chest.

The moment lasted seconds but felt like much longer. "I've missed you too. I can't wait for tomorrow." My lips formed into a smile as I recalled my last client had cancelled their appointment. "But I've good news, I should be at yours by around seven-thirty if the traffic plays ball."

The smile he rewarded me with kept me buoyant right up until I stepped into my family home. The scent of a meat pirog caused my mouth to water and helped settle me a little as childhood memories of my mother teaching me to make the Russian pie, that could be either savoury or sweet, assailed me.

I moved noiselessly down the thick-carpeted hallway to the door at the end that led into a huge, open-plan living area. The kitchen was housed at the back of the house in Kensington, a house my father had refurbed when I was a teenager. It had remained pretty much the same since then.

The furniture was large and comfortable, in an array of reds. The walls were white with a hint of green and held large pictures that showed how beautiful Russia was.

"Ah, you're here. Wonderful timing as always, the pirog is ready. I made your favourite, lamb," Mother called from the kitchen doorway. The smile she gave me showed she had no clue why I was there.

I returned the smile after I swept a glance about the room and didn't find my father. I kissed her cheek and wrapped my arms around her. She hugged me back and the scent of Dior surrounded me.

Only when I pulled back did her brows raise. "What happened?"

"Father is mad I've moved the money out of the trust fund." I didn't beat about the bush as I had no clue when my father would appear.

A light I didn't see often sparked in the depth of my mother's eyes, fury. "That money is yours to do with as you please. It was the whole point of setting up the account. You've always behaved sensibly with money."

There was no stopping the chuckle when I thought about what amounts I'd given away.

"Oh dear, what have you done?" she asked resignedly.

"Let's just say that several well-deserving charities got a great Christmas present."

The smile that formed on her face warmed me, even before she leant in and whispered in my ear, "Good for you, son. He needs these little reminders that money can be used to help those less fortunate."

I hoped she was right.

CHAPTER SIXTEEN

Guy

All night, I watched the clock, unable to concentrate on anything, worrying about Brett. And if I wasn't worrying about him, I was trying to get my head around the fact he was a...*billionaire!*

The jokes I'd aimed at Charlie for falling for a billionaire now seemed to be aimed at me. I wasn't sure quite how to feel about the fact I'd a boyfriend who had more money than...well I didn't know who or what, but two billion was a bloody lot of cash!

"Why are you dancing on that seat? You've been distracted all evening," Charlie pointed out as his head lifted from the corset he was hand stitching. His glasses had slipped to the end of his nose and he looked over the top of them at me.

Was it crass to talk about other people's money? *Brett is not other people, he's your boyfriend.*

"Brett's a billionaire," I blurted out as a wave of heat rode up my neck and caused me to tug at the neck of my sweater.

"He is? Wow, he kept that quiet. I'm sure Griffin doesn't know that about him."

"Oh, please don't say anything." I jumped up off the sofa and started to pace in front of the roaring fire. "I'm not sure I should have said anything. It's just...well...I'm a little..." I trailed off, uncertain how to explain it.

Charlie placed the corset down on the seat of the sofa I'd just vacated and stared up at me. "It's hard. I get it. When I found out just how much Griff is worth, I had moments of doubt. What does he see in me? Does he think I'm only after his money? Would others think I was a money grabber? The money scared me. If I'm honest, it still does. I struggle to see how it's right that one person can have so much when others have so little."

He sighed and a shadow crossed his face. "The thing is, Griffin didn't come from money, far from it. He's worked hard to sustain the empire he inherited. He's also a very generous man who just choses to keep that part hidden and not talk about the charities he supports. He's even bought several houses and turned them into safe havens for abused children." Charlie chewed on his thumbnail as he eyed me with damp eyes.

My heart cinched in my chest as I imagined why Griffin would do that. Had he been abused?

"My advice? If you can, don't let it get between you. Money is a tricky thing when one person has it and the other doesn't. Brett doesn't seem the sort to lord it over others, like some we know."

The scowl he wore was reminiscent of when he'd seen Blake Masters at New Year. "Are you thinking about your good friend Blake?" The guy was a dick of epic portions. He thought his good looks and his father's money could get him anything he wanted. The fact he modelled, and often gave Charlie a hard time, made me instantly dislike him. It hadn't helped that I'd noticed the way he'd eyed Brett with a gleam of possessiveness on New Year's Eve.

"I thought I'd got rid of that monkey off my back, but it seems Blake's father has wheedled in with Maxim to purchase a new hotel in Russia. Griffin wasn't aware of this until after he'd signed the contract. Let's just say if Griffin wasn't in the position of being hit with a huge penalty clause, then he'd have pulled out of the deal." Charlie's hands fluttered in the air. "Anyway, let's not talk about that dick or his father. We were talking about you and Brett."

The pointed look Charlie gave me was enough to get me to return to the sofa. I picked up the nearly finished corset and sighed. "Do you think I'll be enough for Brett?"

I hated the strain in my voice as I admitted aloud the one fear that had come with his confession about the money. Having never had much, it filled me with a strange dread that Maxim would use my lack to make Brett think I wasn't worth his time. My feelings for Brett were too new to know whether the other man felt the same as I did.

"Look at me." When I did as Charlie asked, his face softened. "He's lucky to have you. He knows it too. The way he looks at you, like you hung the moon and the stars, says it all. Trust him. And if that fails, we'll get Nanna and Rachael to sort him out."

I laughed, knowing he'd said it to break the tension, and it worked. "Maybe we need Nanna to have another go at Maxim, set him back on the straight and narrow."

"That might work, but you never know what will happen if Nanna gets involved." Charlie took the corset out of my hands with a dramatic sigh. "Let's get back to work. We both have weekend plans that don't involve sewing or working on course work."

"Amen to that." I eyed the tips of my fingers, which currently resembled a pin cushions, and sagged. Sewing was fast becoming one of my least favourite things to do.

An hour later, I went to bed with the worry still niggling at me. I checked my phone to find no message from Brett. Should I call him? Could he still be with his parents? The last thing I wanted was to call and interrupt something. I dithered for a few minutes as I got ready for bed. Once in bed, I lay against the plump pillows and gave in, sending a brief message.

I hope everything went okay. I can't wait to see you x

The following morning, when I'd woken to find no message from Brett, my worry ramped right back up. Had his father somehow manipulated him into dumping me? I shook my head. *Stop being daft, Brett isn't like that.*

My stomach continued to churn, even with that reassurance, as I showered, dressed, and headed down for breakfast. I had an early class, so I was leaving before Charlie today.

As I entered the kitchen, I halted, seeing Nanna sitting at the kitchen table. "Morning, Nanna, you're up and about early." I got a sinking feeling Charlie might have said something to her after I'd gone to bed when she patted the seat next to her. She gave me a smile I recognised as one my mother often gave me as a teenager when she wanted to have a serious talk.

"Morning, lovely boy, come and sit with me for a minute."

It wasn't a question, so I walked to the table and took the seat she offered. "Charlie spoke to you, didn't he?"

She didn't pretend not to know what I was talking about and nodded. "He did, but it's because he's worried about you, about this situation with Maxim and the...*money*." She all but spat out the last word like it was a swear that tasted bad in her mouth.

"Brett said things have improved between them, yet when he called and dropped this bombshell last night, it seems things have reverted to the way they were before the beginning of the year...I'm worried..." I struggled to voice my own insecurities.

"Listen to me, that man loves you. It's as clear as the nose on your face, my laddie. It's the same for you and you can't deny it."

My lips parted, then shut as my mouth dried at the thought of denying how I felt. I'd been in lust many times before, and I wasn't stupid enough to pretend to myself that my feelings were totally different this time. He lit me up like a bonfire every time I heard his voice or saw his gorgeous, smiling face. If I were completely honest, I'd known the first time we'd met that there'd been more than simple attraction. It was why I'd decided to keep my distance, he had the power to hurt me.

I voiced this to Nanna and her expression became sympathetic. "Life is all about feeling. It's how we know we're alive, lovely boy. Hurting is all part and parcel of loving. There really is no escape, take it from a woman of my years. If I'd found the answer, I'd be as rich as Griff and Brett." She giggled, and deep lines appeared around her mouth and eyes.

"What if I declare my feelings now and he thinks it's because he's told me about the money. Ouch." I snatched my hand away from Nanna after she gave it hard slap. "What was that for?" I complained, rubbing at the back of my now red hand.

"You were being ridiculous, that's what that was for. Do you honestly think Brett doesn't know the difference between a money grabbing arsehole and a genuine person?" She blew out a breath that, if possible, sounded equal measures frustrated and annoyed at the same time.

With my hands in my lap, out of harm's way, I answered truthfully. "Yes, I'm sure he does. But what about Maxim's influence? The man seems to have Brett tied in knots while he's trying to gain his acceptance. He has already threatened Brett over me and, for that matter, told me to back off."

"And did you? Did Brett?" As Nanna pointed out the obvious, my heart thudded painfully against my ribs.

"You think I'm making too much of this, don't you?" I asked resignedly.

Her face softened. "No, I don't. You love him. It's why you're worried. But what you seem to be forgetting is that both you and Brett have stood up to Maxim. That in itself shows that you're already united on that front. Brett might want his father's approval and love, but he's not going to deny his own happiness with you to achieve it." She gave me a confident smile. "I'd bet all of Griff's money on it."

"Why are you betting Griff's money?" came a sleepy voice from the doorway.

Nanna grinned as she turned to Charlie, who was still wearing a pair of shorts and a T-shirt he favoured sleeping in. "Because the man loves me and would give me anything." She fluttered her eyelashes, and I laughed as Charlie snorted.

The door to the annex opened to reveal Rachael and a large, ginger tabby cat. "Fucking feed me," came a maniacal voice, and I jerked.

My eyes widened. "What did you just say, Nanna?"

An innocent expression appeared on her face as Charlie ignored us all to head for the fridge. "I didn't say anything, it was Sissy. She gets very upset if you don't feed her regularly." Nanna leant over and picked up the cat as I glanced at Charlie.

He was standing by the fridge, holding a can of Pepsi. He shrugged as if to say, 'I told you so'. I'd heard about Nanna channelling the cat, but this was the first time I'd witnessed it. Truth be told, I'd thought Charlie and Griff had been pulling my leg. It would seem they hadn't been.

"Nanna, you do know cats can't talk?" I asked tentatively.

A look of disbelief appeared on her face as she shook her head, then glanced at Rachael. "Young people today."

Like I was supposed to understand what that meant, she got up and walked to where Rachael stood. "Let's go and feed Sissy before she starts a ruckus." They headed back through the door Rachael had just come through.

"Fucking feed me," came the maniacal voice again, just as the door closed.

Charlie laughed as he stared at me. "Shut your mouth, you look like you're catching flies."

Unable to stop the laughter, I joined in with Charlie. "Does she really believe it's the cat talking?"

Charlie gave a noncommittal shrug. "Who knows with Nanna." He glanced at the kitchen clock then back at me. "Shouldn't you have already left?"

Checking the time, I cursed as I got up. "Blame Nanna and you."

He blushed and held up his empty hand in a peace offering. "Sorry, I was worried about you. Nanna is much better at giving advice than me." His brow furrowed. "Did I fuck up?"

I sighed. "No, you didn't. But fair warning, when we all go out this weekend, you won't be escaping with excuses of wanting time with Griffin. It's your turn to keep a rein on her."

He shuddered. "I can't say I wasn't pleased to miss teethgate."

I roared with laughter, then clutched my sides as I rocked, tears rolling down my cheeks. "Oh, Brett's face...utterly priceless!"

Charlie chuckled, again checking the time. "I feel I owe you, so if you give me five, I'll give you a lift to uni. That way you shouldn't be too late for your lecture and you can fill me in on Nanna's words of wisdom."

"What," I waited a beat till Charlie had taken a sip of his drink, then I mimicked Nanna's maniacal voice "fucking feed me."

Pepsi fountained out of Charlie's nose as he laughed and spluttered. His eyes streamed as I strolled to him and slapped him on the back, while avoiding the mess on the floor. "I think Brett needs to meet Sissy, don't you?"

Charlie wiped at his chin, then his nose, and shook his head. "You can be evil sometimes, you know that, right?"

"Nah, I'm just a funny Guy."

It took a second for Charlie to register what I'd said, and we both laughed. The laughter continued all the way to uni as we joked and laughed about Griffin's first encounter with Nanna and the cat.

By the time I got to my lecture, I was only fifteen minutes late, and it meant I'd not had time to worry about the continued silence from Brett.

CHAPTER SEVENTEEN

Brett

When I'd woken first thing this morning, with the worst hangover of my life, I'd done something I'd never done in my life; I'd called in sick for work. Then I'd gone back to bed after taking everything I could take to help reduce the jackhammer that was pounding mercilessly at my temples.

That had been five hours earlier, and still I was suffering as I got up to go and shower off the scent of stale alcohol that seemed to permeate from me. What had possessed me to drink vodka with my father? He's fucking Russian!

I shook my head and instantly regretted it when the room wavered for a second. The heat of the water penetrating my skull helped a little, but I still felt like a delicate flower that could break in a stiff breeze as I entered my kitchen ten minutes later.

Heading straight for the coffeemaker, I switched it on, then caught sight of the bakery box my mother had given me to take home last night.

I groaned in delight as I lifted the lid to find several small, sweet-smelling pirogs. Not waiting for the coffee, I practically inhaled two of the pastries when my stomach alerted me to the fact I was starving.

With the third one in my hand, I went to retrieve the cup of coffee that was now ready. I sat at my breakfast bar and sipped at my scalding coffee, I enjoyed the bitterness as the caffeine hit buzzed through me. A triple espresso was the champion of drinks after a heavy drinking session. Not that I had many, and definitely not with my father.

A vague memory of my mother giving my father vodka filtered through my head. Why had I asked for one?

You asked for Dutch courage.

How did that work out for you?

Parts of the conversation returned, and my stomach decided it wasn't so keen on the food and drink I was giving it. I laid the cup and the half-eaten pirog down on the marble countertop. Taking a few deep breaths, I tried to piece together what we'd talked about before I'd ended up drunk in the back of an Uber. Had we talked about the money? The donations to the charities?

The jackhammer at my temples tried to make a new appearance, so I gave up thinking so hard and got up to go and find my phone. I'd ring my mother; it would be far easier than trying to do battle with the fog of alcohol gluing itself to my memories.

After a ten-minute search, I'd had to ring my mobile from the house phone to find it as it had somehow ended up under the bed. How the hell had it got under there?

With no real answer, I stupidly tried again to recall the events of the night before. How could I remember getting home and going to bed, but I couldn't remember other parts of the evening?

Seeing it was futile to try and unlock the secrets of the drunken mind, I clicked my phone open. My heart sank as Guy's name instantly popped up with a message. It was, however, quickly followed by warmth as I read his text.

I hope everything went okay. I can't wait to see you x

Bollocks!

Perching on the edge of the bed, I quickly typed out a message.

I'm sorry. I've just seen this message. I'll explain everything when I see you later. I should be at Griffin's about five xx

173

There was not even a second before my screen showed the message had been read, so I waited when the icon showed Guy was typing.

I was concerned about you. I might have to spank your arse for making me worry ;) Can't wait to see you, sweets x

A flood of desire spread through my lower body and I shifted on the bed. I'd been spanked playfully in the past, and though I'd enjoyed it, I can't say I'd actively sought out a partner that was into it. Thoughts of Guy spanking me dressed in his thigh-high boots were something I appeared to totally get on board with if my body's reaction was anything to go by.

This, however, was not news, because whenever Guy was on my mind, the feelings that often accompanied those thoughts were desire. Only lately, they were complemented by something else...love. I'd experienced love before, so I knew what I felt and, if memory served me right, I might have told my parents that last night...I think.

It didn't matter whether I had or hadn't, what I did know was that I wanted to declare those feelings to Guy.

I scratched at my bristly chin as I eyed the phone screen that had Guy's picture as my wallpaper. His smile radiated such warmth and love as I recalled the urge I'd had to snap the picture while we were FaceTiming. His blue-grey eyes seemed to bore into me and make me believe that this time, love wouldn't kick my arse like it had in the past.

Yesterday for me had been a pivotal moment when I'd rung Guy first, after my father had upset me. Normally I'd have rung Luke, my best friend. In the past, I'd never gone to any of my previous boyfriends, even the long-term ones, to talk about my issues with my father. Why was Guy so different? Does it matter?

What are you going to do about it, more to the point?

A buzz started in my ears as my heart took flight at what I wanted to do, but whether I had the courage was something else. My fingers trembled as I clutched at my phone and stood to go and pack my weekend bag.

The traffic out of London on a Friday afternoon was brutal, and any hopes of getting to Griffin's home earlier than planned was sabotaged by an accident on the motorway that had traffic backed up for miles.

When I eventually pulled into Griffin's drive, I was hungry and feeling rather grumpy as the tail end of the hangover tried to cling on. I'd only a second to grab my bag before the door opened and Guy rushed out.

His face was flushed with happiness as he jogged to me and straight away wrapped me in a big hug. I buried my face in his sweet-smelling neck and clung on, trying to avoid dropping my bag on the wet ground.

The hug went on and on, soothing the remaining raw edges I'd carried since the day before. "You give the best hugs," I muttered against his neck.

He chuckled. "That was my 'Drag Queen who hasn't seen her favourite twink in ages because he stopped working at the bar, but he came in specially this week to see her perform' hug. Did it make you feel better?" he asked in all seriousness.

And though I laughed at the description, my heart melted at the love shining from his face. "I love you." Furious heat spread up my neck at how the words just tumbled from my mouth.

There was no chance for me to say more as my mouth was claimed in a kiss that would clearly register on the Richter scale. It shook my world, and my bag tumbled to the wet ground with the need to hold on to him.

His mouth was hot and wet as he deepened the kiss, giving me no time to think, only feel. Desire flared through my body and I was rock hard in seconds, causing waves of dizziness to make my legs tremble. Heat from his body penetrated through my waterproof jacket, and I could all but feel the steam rising between us as my breathable jacket failed to do its job.

"Put him down, dear lord, my heart. I think you've melted my panties clean off," came Agnes's voice, somewhere behind us.

The heat now riding my cheeks, as I struggled to take a breath, was all to do with embarrassment. Guy didn't seem to be too bothered as he held on to me for another moment, his eyes full of promises. Then he mouthed quietly, "later" before he let me go.

He bent to retrieve what was surely a soaked bag with the amount of water on the ground, while I prayed the leather was sturdy enough to have kept my clothes dry.

"You know it's naughty to pry, Nanna." Guy's voice was full of humour as he took my hand and led me towards the open door.

I gave a surreptitious glance down to check my jacket hid my arousal.

Nanna looked unrepentant as she gave me a beaming smile. "I was just coming to say hello to Brett. Is it my fault you decided to check his tonsils were still present?"

I choked on my laughter, whereas Guy just tutted as she stepped out of our way and allowed us to pass.

"It's a good job I love you," he muttered, as he continued towards the stairs.

Was he talking to Agnes or me? It had to be Agnes, right? A worm of uncertainty crept past the desire still pulsing through me from the kiss he'd given me.

He'd not answered my declaration, had he? *He kissed you senseless.* Yes, but was that because he didn't want to answer me?

"Whatever is going on in the pretty head of yours?" Guy asked, the second he shut the bedroom door. He dropped my bag on the floor and his fingertip traced the furrow between my eyes. One I'd not realised was there till he touched it.

"I...you never..." I growled in frustration. I was nearly bloody forty and I was acting like a tongue-tied teenager. *Spit it out!*

The air in my lungs backed up as he moved and I found myself pressed against the door, his lips millimetres from mine. His gaze held mine for what felt like eons, as my heart beat wildly in my chest, before he whispered, "I love you too."

His mouth captured mine in a kiss that was just as potent as the one he'd given me outside, but with a difference. This one was a sweet exploration, and though it held passion, it was love that seemed to be the underlying feel of it. I melted against the door and rejoiced in the feel of him pressed against me, surrounding me with his love.

"I love you," he breathed it against my lips as one kiss blended with another and time faded away.

My chest felt like it was going to burst with joy as he made love to my mouth. I'd always enjoyed being kissed, but Guy seemed to treat my mouth like his favourite delicacy as he moaned and took his fill.

When his mouth moved to my neck, my lips felt sensitive and I felt on the brink of coming, I was so aroused. "Your mouth, dear gods," I whispered breathlessly as he continued to explore my neck until he reached the collar of my jacket.

A hot chuckle ghosted over my skin as he eased back. His heavy-lidded gaze met mine. "You are far too tempting, and I seem to forget myself."

He went to step back, but I refused to let him go. "Please, don't stop, I'm so close," I spoke honestly, desperate for more. I ground my lower body against him, causing his nostrils to flare.

"Could you come from just me kissing you?" he rasped as he gave a sexy swivel of his hips. His cock pressed firmly against mine.

"I think if you fucking blew on me right now, I could come," I gasped.

"Is that so?" I didn't understand the gleam in his eyes until he let go of me to kneel at my feet, his hands going for the belt of my jeans. I sucked in a shaky breath as he undid my jeans and seconds later pulled out my cock.

Trembles shook my body at the intent on his face as his mouth opened and the heat of his breath bathed the wet tip of my cock. "Oh fuck!"

CHAPTER EIGHTEEN

Guy

S mug satisfaction filled me at proving to Brett
that I could indeed make him come without
actually touching him. I might have cheated
by talking dirty as I blew on his cock, but hey, I'm
competitive. He still looked a little shell-shocked
when, hand in hand, we walked into the kitchen
twenty minutes after we'd gone upstairs. The taste
of him lingered on my tongue and I'd been all right
with that until I spied Nanna sat at the table.

Warmth crawled up my chest and neck as she
gave me a look that indicated that she was aware
we'd been up to naughtiness. Why had I thought it
was a good idea to come down and order pizza?

I swallowed a sigh as Brett's fingers tightened
around mine and I glanced at him to see a
matching redness creeping up his neck.

"You're looking a little flushed there, boys?" Nanna's eyes sparkled with mirth as I shook my head at her.

"Give over Nanna and stop trying to embarrass us."

There was the sound of a door opening, followed by the thud of feet on the stairs.

"Griff's home then." Nanna pointed out the obvious as Charlie made a whooping noise in the hallway.

Her hands rubbed together as she gave me and Brett a shrewd look. "So, what are our plans for the weekend?"

My brows rose. "Our plans?" I pointed between me and Brett. "You do mean this 'our', right?" I asked with a sinking heart.

"Guy, you know you want me to come along. You have the best fun then."

I held up my free hand as Brett started to laugh. "I'm just going to say *teethgate*!"

She did have the courtesy to blush, but that didn't seem to stop the light of determination from dying in her eyes. "Yes, well, I've been and bought some Fixodent so that shouldn't be an issue." Her head tilted and she gave me a winning smile. "Now, I'm sure you and Brett have a lot of catching up to do tonight. So I know what to pull out of my wardrobe, where will we be going tomorrow night? I heard you mention Legends to Charlie?"

I was saved, or so I thought, when Charlie walked in the room with Griffin. His tie was slightly askew, and his lips were puffy, like Charlie had attacked them.

"Oh, Griff, you've just made it in time to help decide where we're all going to tomorrow night. I believe Charlie and Guy mentioned Legends. What do you think?"

Griffin, who'd clearly not picked up on Charlie's alarmed expression, nodded at Nanna. "Legends is good if that's where everyone wants to go. I'm not bothered."

It was only when Griffin glanced at Charlie's 'are you for real' expression, that he seemed to figure out he'd walked straight into Nanna's trap.

He gave a heartfelt sigh as he glanced back at Nanna. "You conned me," he gritted out, sounding more resigned than angry.

"I've no clue what you're meaning. Anyway, I better go tell Rachael we've got plans for tomorrow." As she spoke, she slid off the chair and started to head to the annex door. A second after she opened the door, Sissy appeared.

I clamped my lips together, knowing full well what was coming next.

"Fucking feed me," the maniacal voice screeched.

Griffin sighed, Charlie rolled his eyes, and Brett jerked much like I had done the first time I'd heard her channel the cat. Brett's gaze swept the room when no one said anything as Nanna disappeared through the door, the cat at her heels.

The look on his face was too much and the laughter poured out.

"Why...what...oh dear," Brett muttered, his face turning a shade of red that wasn't very flattering.

"What's wrong?" I choked out past the laughter.

Brett's brow furrowed deeply as his gaze again swept the room, as if he were trying to figure out why the occupants in the room didn't seem bothered by Nanna's odd behaviour. "What was she doing?"

A snigger came from Charlie before he spoke. "She's channelling the cat. You should ask Griff about his first encounter with Nanna and Sissy." His eyes gleamed with humour as he wrapped his arm around Griffin's waist and laid his head on his broad shoulder.

"Don't remind me." His smile was warm and full of love as he looked at Charlie. "It's a memory I've chosen to bury deep in the vault of my mind, never to be unearthed again." He shuddered for affect as he glanced at Brett and me. "She traumatised me."

"Hey, at least she didn't drug you," Charlie pointed out, laughing, which caused Brett to frown.

"I'll fill you in later, sweets. But right now, my stomach thinks my throat has been cut. I'm starved as I missed breakfast and lunch. You two fancy pizza? I was going to have it delivered."

With a resounding yes, I ordered enough pizza to fill everyone and still have leftovers. Charlie and Griffin disappeared, giving me time to sit Brett down and talk about the day before.

A sense I was missing something lingered when he'd finished talking. "You didn't ring your Mum to find out what was said?" I asked, hating how uncertain I sounded.

He sighed. "I was going to, then I found your message, and all I wanted to do was come here to see you." His cheeks pinked as he lifted his gaze from the table he'd been focused on. "I wanted to tell you how I felt, to maybe see—"

The doorbell sounded and I cursed. "You were going to say something?" I pushed as I stood.

"No, it's fine, it can wait. Go get the pizza." There was a sound of movement above us, so I did as he asked, promising myself we'd talk about whatever was on his mind later.

Rushing to get out of the spitting rain, we made our way up the steps that lead onto the patio in front of Legends. In the summer it was a beautiful, sun-drenched terrace, but right now it served only as a smoking area for a couple of damp-looking drunks.

Charlie and I greeted Soloman, the burly bouncer with the widest smile I've ever seen, who ushered us straight in, ignoring the angry protests from the rowdy hen party that were being made to wait outside.

Making our way through the glass double doors, we entered the large open-plan bar. They'd recently refurbished the whole place, and the new cream and blue colour scheme, though a little muted compared to what we were used to, was offset nicely by the portraits of Drag legends, all backlit in bright fuchsia.

The place was pretty full, being a Saturday night, making the room feel noisy but alive. Of course, this was helped by all the gay classics that were playing in the background. Up here in the bar, the music was all picked by the bar staff, so it was as camp and as cheesy as you like. If you wanted anything else, you had to go downstairs to the cramped little club they had, but even that was a little touch and go, depending on who was DJing.

As we weaved our way to the bar with the order of drinks, Griffin took Charlie, Nanna, and Rachael to the empty table he'd spotted while Brett stayed with me to help carry the drinks.

After I'd placed the order, I glanced at him and smiled, trying to decide if I should bring up the conversation we'd not finished the previous day before the pizza had arrived. He'd been beat last night, and stuffed with pizza, he'd snuggled into me on the sofa and struggled to stay awake, so I'd let it be. This morning, I'd woken to find him sucking my brains out of my cock, making it impossible to think about anything. Then we'd spent some time with Nanna before going for a long walk. I'd nudged at him, hoping he'd open up, but when he'd remained tight-lipped, I'd got a sinking feeling that whatever was ever on his mind, he'd decided to keep quiet about it.

No amount of second guessing helped to garner me an answer to what was going on in his head. There was definitely something, as he was distracted. So much so he'd made no comment about my outfit, which was unlike him.

I'd taken particular care to dress, knowing we'd go downstairs later to dance. My simple black polo shirt fit me perfectly, and I'd tucked it into my crisp white skinny jeans to help accentuate my waist. The black belt and simple silver chain necklace were the only accessories I wore, allowing my black, metal studded, eight-inch stiletto calf boots to really stand out.

The busy bar made it hard to have a conversation without someone overhearing us, so I let it be, even as my stomach twisted with anxiety.

"What was the last drink you wanted?" the cute bartender asked as he placed all but Nanna's drink on the bar in front of us.

Brett laughed as I mumbled to the guy, "A porn star martini, please." When the guy wandered off, I glanced at Brett. "She does it on purpose, I swear."

"At least we're not eating tonight."

I matched his smile. "That's a good point."

A minute later, the bartender returned and placed the drink with the others.

When I went to hand over my credit card, Brett shook his head. "I'll get this. You paid for the pizza last night."

My heart skipped a beat as I was suddenly reminded that my man could afford anything his heart desired. An urge to argue was taken away when his lips brushed against mine in a sweet kiss.

His eyes held mine as he whispered, "It's only money, please don't let it come between us."

There was a hint of fear in his voice that stopped me cold. Was that what I was going to do? As I stared at him, I acknowledged that was exactly what I'd been about to do. "I'm sorry, you're right. It shouldn't be an issue."

His brow rose. "But?"

I sighed and kissed his mouth. "I don't want you ever to think I told you I love you just because you're loaded."

It was his turn to sigh. "I know that I'm worth more than the money, as are you." His lips again pressed against mine. "We'll figure it out—"

"Erm, do you want a receipt?" the bartender asked, breaking the sudden tension between us.

Drinks in hand, we walked back to the table, and I sent up a silent wish that money would not be our downfall.

CHAPTER NINETEEN

Brett

Monday evening, I got in my car to drive to my parents' home. Knots of tension in my shoulders throbbed as I weaved through the late-evening traffic.

I couldn't remember the last time I'd visited them twice in one week. The blank spots in my memory had continued to plague me after my conversation with Guy. He had given me a sceptical look when I couldn't answer all his questions about how things were now between my father and me, so I'd bitten the bullet and cancelled my dinner plans with Luke and Scott this evening.

One more thing I was going to have to add to the list of things to rearrange and fit into my crammed calendar. After taking Friday off, I'd had

Chloe go through my appointment book to shoehorn in the appointments I'd missed. That meant there was little time, even in the evening, to do anything. This added to the problem of trying to see my best friend and his fiancé. Our schedules weren't as flexible as they used to be. Luke managed The Worthington and kept odd hours, especially when there were big functions in the hotel. This time of year, it seemed there was one on every day. Scott, his fiancé, was no different as head waiter at the Flamingo Bar. They could have gone to dinner this coming weekend, but I'd promised Guy I'd head back to Brighton again, so I'd had to decline the offer.

It had been hard to leave him early this morning, and for the first time in my memory, I'd not wanted to go to work. I blew out a sigh as I looked in the rear-view mirror before indicating to switch lanes and turn up the road towards my parents' Kensington home. My heart sank into my boots as the house came into view. The place was lit up like a Christmas tree and the drive was full of cars.

"Fuck!" I muttered as I considered if I should drive back home or stop. My hand reached for the indicator when I spotted a lone parking spot. The universe seemed to want me to go in.

As I got out of the car, into the bitterly cold evening air, I inhaled. The iciness left me struggling to take another breath as I pulled my wool coat closer to my body. The lights on my car flashed as the locks engaged and I headed to the front door. Using my door key, I entered and was met with a wall of warm, scented air and chatter. With no time to decide to leave, my mother appeared and her face lit up.

"I wasn't sure you'd come."

My eyes widened. Crap, what had I agreed to? "You know if I agree to come, then I will," I hedged, plastering a smile on my face as my mother held out her hand to take my coat.

"That may be so, but your Father's business investors aren't your normal cup of tea, are they? Just don't let them talk you into investing, remember what I said on Friday."

I swallowed a groan of despair. "Refresh my memory."

She tweaked the end of my nose, a habit she'd had when I was little. "Don't let the need to please your father be the reason you agree to something. You made great progress last week. I was half-expecting you to bring Guy tonight, to prove that you're serious about proposing to him."

A wave of dizziness washed over me, and I swayed on the spot. Had I told my parents I was going to ask Guy to marry me? Holy fuck! The look on my mother's face seemed to say I had. What is it they say about a drunk person, they speak the truth?

My heart thumped painfully against my ribs, and what I'd wanted to talk to Guy about, that I'd avoided, sprung into my mind. Living together was one thing, getting engaged was an entirely different matter. Was I ready for that?

You love him.

That I did, and I got the distinct impression after this morning, that my feelings for Guy would only deepen the more time we spent together.

"Oh, there you are, Hannah, can you..." My father pulled up short when he saw me standing in the hallway. What appeared to be pleasure covered his face. "You made it." His voice thickened.

"Yes," I replied, at a loss and trying to figure out what on earth I'd said that put that look on his face. I'd been convinced he'd be...actually, I was clueless about how he'd be because I couldn't recall what I'd said.

Whatever foresight I'd had to get me here tonight, I hoped it continued to help me out as I was ushered into the packed living room. I nodded to several people I knew as my father guided me to...oh fuck!

Blake Masters gave me a once over that made my skin crawl. The man might be attractive, but it didn't go past the outer layer. I used my fake party smile as my father introduced me to the group of men who were standing with Blake.

I listened to the talk about a hotel that I was sure Griffin had opted to invest in. My gaze swept the room, half-expecting to see him. I was disappointed to find he wasn't there.

As the conversation continued, I zoned out, going back over what my mother had said in the hall. Had I really told my parents I was going to marry Guy? I started to daydream about the wedding. Would Guy want a big wedding with all the pomp and ceremony, or would he prefer a select wedding in some far-off destination? I'd always imagined myself on a white sandy beach with close friends when I tied the knot. I'd never got to the planning stage with Nigel, he'd wanted an expensive ring but nothing more.

What kind of ring would Guy like? I recalled the pieces of jewellery he'd worn when we'd been together. Classy for sure.

"Are you planning to go to Munich next month?"

I blinked owlishly at Blake, doing my best to stop a flush riding up my neck. "No, I've no plans for any holidays."

His sculpted brows rose. "If you're investing in the hotel, surely you'll be coming." He laid a possessive hand on my arm and squeezed. "It will be a great opportunity to spend some time together, without *those* people who don't fit in our circle—"

I shook the hand off my arm. "Those people would be who? My boyfriend? He's the kind of people I like in my *circle*." I kept my voice low so the men around us didn't hear me. "My time off is precious, and I prefer to spend it with people *I actually like*." It was rude and possibly uncalled for, but the look on his face and the innuendo got my back up.

If I weren't mistaken, he'd seen me and Guy together over the New Year. And even if I wasn't with Guy, this man was the last person I'd want to be with. He had social-climber written all over him.

Before he could respond, I touched my father's arm as I leant into him. "I'm just going to get a drink."

He glanced at Blake, his expression unfathomable, then he met my gaze, his eyes sparking with humour. "As long as it's not vodka," he murmured before answering a question one of the other men had aimed at him.

My father had just made a joke at my expense! I chuckled as I walked off.

Even though the evening hadn't been what I'd planned, besides the interlude with Blake, I had a good time and avoided the alcohol. I'd also managed to evade getting into a situation where anyone could ask me to invest my money.

What I did learn was that there were several men connected to my father who'd invested in new businesses related to the clothing market, and it got me thinking. Would Guy and Charlie be interested in a silent business partner?

Charlie was the more business-minded of the two of them. It appeared he'd used his contacts in the modelling world to access and purchase all the cast-off clothes from fashion shows at a reduced rate. They'd used the expensive materials for upcycling and creating the new pieces that Guy designed. The ethos behind it showed a lot of thought and understanding about the planet today and the high number of clothes rotting in landfill.

My father's eyes gleamed with what looked like pride as I'd talked about their concept for their clothing range and the ethos behind the business. I'd garnered several business cards to give to the men by the time I was ready to leave.

In a flurry of goodbyes, I made my escape with a promise to my mother to bring Guy for dinner. At home, later that night, I stretched out on my bed and let my mind wonder.

Was it a good thing to mix business with pleasure? Charlie and Guy could use some of the money I had to start their business. It was a solid investment.

Had Griffin offered Charlie money? They'd not mentioned anything when they'd talked about it. I searched my memory. Had Griffin been present when they'd talked about the business? Yes, I was sure he had been.

I tapped at my lip and my eyes narrowed in thought. Was it overstepping if I spoke to Griffin?

CHAPTER TWENTY

Guy

"**W**hy are you frowning at the computer like that?" I asked Charlie as I plonked my backside down on the chair next to him.

We'd only got home an hour ago, and we were supposed to eat, then have another marathon sewing session with Nanna and Rachael. They really had been a godsend. Nanna was a genius with a needle and thread. Better than Charlie, not that I'd say that aloud if I wanted to remain friends. Rachael was great too, though she didn't have the same flare that Nanna had.

The fashion show was planned for four weeks' time, and Charlie had managed to wangle a well-known photographer, Marcus Crestwell, to take pictures for us. Charlie was a huge fan of Marcus's.

He'd bought two of his books of artwork. I could see he was a genius behind the camera. Some of the pictures he'd taken in war-torn countries ripped your heart right out.

I'd questioned why he did high-end fashion shoots then went off to countries with the risk of being hurt or worse, killed. Charlie hadn't a clue and said he'd been too flustered to ask him anything personal. Apparently, Griffin got all possessive when Marcus had flirted with him the one time he'd photographed Charlie.

"I've had a couple of emails—"

"Why does that have you frowning," I questioned in confusion.

"If you let me finish," he rolled his eyes at me as he peered over the rim of his glasses, "they're looking to meet to talk about possible investment in our business."

I got up and walked behind Charlie to look at the screen, my stomach flipflopping with excitement. "Have you put out feelers for investment?"

We'd talked about it after Charlie had declined Griffin's generous offer to fund us. Charlie had been clear he didn't want to mix business with pleasure. He'd confessed, after Griffin had left us to talk about his offer, that he was worried it might put a strain on their relationship if we failed, and I'd agreed with him. As much as the investment would have solved the immediate issue of financing the business, getting your boyfriend involved was only asking for trouble.

He glanced over his shoulder at me and what I saw caused me to tense. "No, I picked up several loan applications for small businesses."

Had Brett had a hand in this? "Do you think Brett might have had something to do with this?"

Charlie's eyes narrowed before he looked back at the screen. "I was actually thinking it might have been Griffin, but it could be Brett too. Let's Google these companies and see what pops up."

Charlie's fingers flew over the keyboard.

About an hour later, I glanced blearily up at Nanna when she questioned, "Aren't we sewing this evening?"

Lost in reading all the information Charlie had printed off while he'd continued to search for a connection to Griffin or Brett, I'd forgotten the time. "Yeah, we are. We just got a little caught up."

I smiled at Rachael as she appeared, carrying a sewing basket and holding several items of clothing she'd been working on. "Oh my god, have you finished those already?" I dropped the papers I held that up to now, we'd found nothing obvious, to go and see what Rachael was carrying.

"Why, of course, I have. These were a real pleasure to work on." She placed everything down on the chair beside her, then picked back up a silk top in cerise that had been hand painted with gorgeous, bold green and yellow flowers. It was cut to fit under the bust and flare out over problem areas such as the hips and stomach. She wore a look of pure appreciation as she made it swirl.

"That would look great on you." The second the words were out of my mouth, Nanna's head shot up.

"You could wear it at the fashion show. I'm going to go with the long floral caftan."

It was Charlie's head that came up next as he pinned Nanna with a horrified expression. "No way, Nanna."

She tutted at him and looked at me. I immediately had the urge to take cover, knowing I was defenceless against her.

"This show is about showing the versatility of the pieces you've designed, right?"

I nodded reluctantly, sensing where this was leading.

"What's more versatile than two ladies in their prime, showcasing your fashions?" She grinned at Rachael. "We'll look like real bobby dazzlers in these, won't we, Rachael? We'll wow the crowds so much, you'll find yourselves inundated with orders. You mark my words, Charlie boy."

I glanced at Charlie, his shoulders sagging as he blew out a breath of what appeared to be resignation. "One outfit each, and you don't interfere in the show, got it?" He pointed at Nanna, then at Rachael. "I mean it."

I clamped my lips together while struggling to keep my laughter at bay. Charlie shot me a hard look and I was lost. Laughter peeled out of me as Nanna patted Charlie on the shoulder saying, "We'll behave, we promise." It was too much, and Charlie glanced heavenward, his face revealing he wasn't fooled for one second.

Once the hilarity was over, I noticed Nanna had picked up the papers I'd been reading. "What's all this?" she asked.

"Charlie had a couple of emails from companies showing an interest in investing in our business. We're just doing a bit of research on them to see who owns the businesses."

Her brows rose, but she said nothing as she went back to reading the pages.

Rachael sat and started to sew as Charlie went back to reading whatever was on his screen. About to take a seat next to Rachael, I stopped as Nanna spoke.

"This company, Sak Way, is connected to Maxim. I'm sure I heard him talking about it with one of the men he was with in St. Moritz."

As if she hadn't just dropped a bomb on me, she carried on talking, but I heard nothing as I met

Charlie's now wide-eyed shock. Convinced I looked no better, I struggled to swallow past the dryness in my mouth.

Charlie broke eye contact first as he shifted his stare to Nanna. "Are you sure?" His voice sounded strained to me, but I was trying to figure out what Maxim's game was. What was Maxim up to? Did he want to set me up? Was it bribery to make me leave Brett alone?

"I'm pretty sure," she thumbed her lip as her eyes became unfocused. "Yes, he clearly told Rupert the Dickweed that he'd diversified into fashion. Griffin was there, I'm sure he can confirm it." Nanna looked pleased with herself as she beamed at me, then Charlie. "See, it looks like Maxim has come to his senses after all."

I wasn't so sure of that, and judging by the look on Charlie's face, neither was he. "Let's leave it for now. Griff is back from Madrid tomorrow. I'll talk to him about it then."

"Okay." I shifted my gaze to Nanna, not wanting to think about what Maxim's motives were. "Dickweed?"

She gave a bark of laughter. "Yes, didn't you think that Rupert guy looked a bit like a weed and he was a dick? I think it suits him." She winked at me. "So did Brett."

Chuckling, I winked back at Nanna. "That's because my boyfriend isn't stupid."

Doing my best to ignore the nerves fluttering around inside me, I sat with Rachael as I clocked the time. The night was getting away from us, and with my weekend already planned, I couldn't afford to spend time worrying, so I pushed it aside in favour of keeping my mind busy.

That lasted until I shut my bedroom door and all the anxiety returned, right along with the unanswered questions.

Did Brett know about what his father was up to? I undressed, then slipped on my jersey pants while I chewed my lower lip between my teeth. The possibility of sleep seemed unlikely with my mind whirring, and the following day I had a full class schedule.

Seeing no way out, I sat on the edge of my bed and dialed Brett.

His voice came through the speaker, but the screen was black. "Hello."

I cursed at how sleepy he sounded. "Shit, I'm sorry, I've woken you."

"Don't apologise, I'm glad you've woken me."

I chuckled at the obvious lie as a lamp was switched on and he appeared on the screen looking sleep tousled.

Warmth spread through me as he gave me a beautiful smile and, for a second, I contemplated keeping quiet.

CHAPTER TWENTY-ONE

Brett

As I blinked at Guy, it took a moment to register the frown marring his brow. Then it smoothed out and I rubbed at my eyes to clear my vision, wondering if I'd imagined it.

"Are you okay? Did something happen?" As I asked, I shifted to sit up against the headboard to get comfortable. I tried to clear the sleep from my mind and recall if we'd planned to talk tonight when we'd spoken yesterday. I'd had two late-evening clients booked, so as far as I could remember, the plan was to talk Thursday evening.

The silence stretched, taking my nerves along with it when a resigned look appeared on Guy's face.

"Did you tell your father about the business idea Charlie and I have?"

His voice held a wealth of hesitancy and I was instantly alert. The air seemed to trap itself in my lungs as Monday night ran through my head. "Yes, I did. What did he do?" This time I was sure I was the one wearing a resigned expression when Guy's face became pinched.

"He sent Charlie an email expressing a wish to invest in our business." He said it in such a rush that it took me a moment to unravel the words.

"He did?" I asked in alarm. "He never mentioned anything about it to me." I didn't miss the look of relief that crossed Guy's face before he narrowed his eyes.

"What do you think his game is?"

I signed and rubbed at my face. "To be honest, I've no clue. My father isn't frivolous with his money. He only invests in businesses he feels will make money."

"Really?" The relief on Guy's face was now replaced by disbelief.

"Yes, really. My father hasn't made billions of pounds by not being a shrewd businessman," I snapped, then instantly regretted it when Guy masked his feelings with a blank expression. "I'm sorry. I shouldn't have used that tone. It's just regardless of my father's shortcomings, he has always been an honourable businessman. You'll be hard pressed to find anything that suggests his business methods are underhanded. He's always honest, even brutally so at times."

Guy's chest heaved as he sighed. "I'm sorry, it's just hard to align the man who threatened me to keep away from his son, with the man now offering to fund mine and Charlie's business."

"I'll talk to him...better still, why don't you come and talk to him. I was going to mention at the weekend that my parents have invited us to dinner."

Guy's brows tried to disappear up his forehead as he eyed me like I'd lost my marbles. "Dinner with your parents," he squeaked.

I chuckled. "Yes, and I promise they won't have you for dinner, but I can't promise the same." I left it hanging there as a slash of pink coated his cheeks.

"Is that right? I'll get the train up to London after I'm finished at uni. Will that work?"

My heart triple-timed against my ribs as I nodded. I'd make it work, with the look Guy was aiming at me.

"Could you slack off Friday and stay with me this weekend?" I held my breath, expecting a denial with the fashion show looming.

His head tilted to the side and my toes curled into the sheet as he spoke. "Oh, I think that can be arranged. Just think, we'll be able to make as much noise as we want." He gave me a devilishly killer smile. "I hope your apartment has soundproofing."

A shiver of desire ran through me as I licked my lips. "It does."

"Then I'll look forward to you shouting my name until you're hoarse."

This time I squirmed as my cock started to plump. "That's just cruel. How am I supposed to get back to sleep now?"

"Just know I'll be in the same predicament." The grin he gave me left me breathless and, shortly after, he finished the call with plans for me to meet him at the station nearest to Kensington.

After switching off the light, I lay against my plump pillows and I stared up at the inky black. What was my father up to?

I cursed, recalling I'd yet again forgotten to pump my mother for information about the week before and what I'd said to my father in my drunken state.

What was I letting myself in for, going in unarmed with Guy? It was too late to call him back and say I'd changed my mind about tomorrow.

I shut my eyes and prayed I wasn't leading us both into the lion's den.

Part excitement, part anxiety ran through me at how easy it had been to arrange dinner tonight with my parents. I entered the train station and remained by the entrance, waiting for Guy to appear. He'd messaged to say his train was on time, so I headed out of the office early and got an Uber to meet him.

I'd not been able to move any clients the next day, but Guy hadn't seemed too bothered when he said he could go and people watch on London's South Bank.

People rushed everywhere I looked as I watched for Guy. The movement and noise were constant. I held my phone in my clammy hand just in case Guy couldn't find me. I didn't want to miss his call.

The air caught in my lungs as I caught sight of him walking through the crowd. He certainly stood out. The suit trousers he wore were a deep navy-blue, embroidered with a floral design in shades of gold, muted pinks, and reds. They hugged his legs perfectly, and the silky looking material seemed to flow over him as he glided towards me on a pair of leather knee-high boots in the same blue as the trousers. I couldn't quite judge the height from where I was standing, but the platform on them looked considerable. Despite the cold, he wore nothing but a tight black vest up top, the suit jacket slung over his arm, but neither of them were what drew my gaze.

His neck was enveloped in a gorgeous choker, bands of tight-fitting white crystals wrapping around his delicate skin. Three strings of crystals then travelled from it, one down the centre of his chest, and one down to loop under each arm. These were then connected in an intricate design of crystals that wrapped his torso in a glittering spiderweb.

I wasn't sure what my parents would think of how he looked, but right then, I couldn't have cared less. This man had chosen me, had declared his love, and dressed as he was, he was making his point clear. Accept me, or fuck off. The choice for me was the easiest of my life. The daydreaming I'd done about proposing flooded my mind. Was it too soon?

I wasn't wholly sure of the answer, with one exception: my heart. It already belonged to this man and nothing was going to change that.

Guy's coloured lips moved into a stunning smile as he stopped in front of me, towering over me. "Hello, gorgeous, are you looking for a hot date?"

A woman in her twenties, with rainbow hair, grinned at us as she walked past. "If he's not interested, I'll take you up on the offer."

I placed a possessive hand on his arm, my brow arching. "Do I look like a fool to you?"

She laughed and shook her head. "Can't blame a girl for trying." With that, she disappeared into the night.

"Another dream shattered," Guy stated in a dramatic tone as he slipped his arm around my waist and pulled me into his body. His lips brushed softly against mine. "Now *your* dreams, I plan to make come true."

A shiver of desire ran through me and I sent up a silent prayer that he meant what he said. "I'll hold you to that," I whispered against his lips before I eased back. "Aren't you cold?"

"A little, but as I've always said, if you aren't in at least a little discomfort, you probably don't look *fabulous,*" he replied with a grin.

"I'll take your word on that," I laughed, gazing up at him. "So, are you ready to meet the parents...*officially*?"

His eyes gleamed, and I was uncertain how to read his expression as he took my hand. Had he got my meaning?

"More than. Let's get this show on the road." He tugged me gently towards the exit and I sucked in a shaky breath.

Please let my father behave himself.

CHAPTER TWENTY-TWO

Guy

By the time we reached Brett's parents' home, the difference in our upbringing had become very obvious. The houses we passed were in the tens of millions of pounds bracket, nothing at all like the small two-up two-down I'd been raised in. It wasn't often that I felt intimidated, but right now, as we walked up to the palatial-looking home belonging to Brett's parents, I felt the nerves kick in.

When I'd got dressed to impress earlier this evening, I'd hoped it would give me a confidence boost, yet as Brett opened the front door and ushered me inside the house, I was struggling not to show how anxious I was feeling. My hands were icy cold as they balled at my sides.

The marble floor was slippy and I eyed it with trepidation.

"Brett, Guy, how lovely to see you both," exclaimed Hannah, who appeared from a door at the end of the long hallway, followed by the scent of some delicious food. Her blonde hair was styled into chic, tousled curls around her youthful face. She wore a bare minimum of make-up and had on a pair of simple dark-brown skirt and a burnt-orange silk shirt that gave her face a lovely warm glow.

I could see the similarities between her and Brett as she smiled and stopped in front of us.

"Hello, Mother," Brett stepped into her open arms and kissed her cheek before he shifted to hold his hand out to me, beckoning me closer. "I'd like to officially introduce you to my boyfriend, Guy Finchley."

My heart stuttered in my chest at the pride in his voice. Hannah held out her hand and I took it. "So lovely to meet you, officially."

Her laughter tinkled like tiny bells. "The pleasure is mine. You're like a breath of fresh air, and how you make my boy glow is wonderful—"

"Mother, please." Brett groaned in complaint, his cheeks pinking.

The sound of heavy footsteps had us all turning to look back down the hallway. Maxim was dressed a little more formally than his wife, in a charcoal-grey suit and tie. The shirt, a pale grey, stretched to fit his broad chest. He was so large compared to Brett, I struggled to see any resemblance between them.

His gaze swept me from head to foot, but he kept his thoughts masked as he held out his hand. "It's good to see you, Guy."

He sounded genuine so I took the hand in a firm grip and shook it. "Thank you for inviting me to dinner." I left it at that, unable to say it was good to see him with my stomach trying to limbo dance under a bar sitting an inch off the ground.

In no time at all, we'd been ushered into a formal dining room I was sure could rival one in Buckingham Palace. The long, hardwood table gleamed with a perfect shine, as did all the glass and silverware sat on it. The rich scent of food mixed with polish and perfume as we sat in plush leather seats.

Brett's expression was strained as he eyed his parents, now sat opposite us eating silently. The tension was so thick, I'd swear I could cut it with the steak knife I held.

Long minutes passed as we ate what I'm sure was delicious food, but tasted like sawdust in my mouth as no one spoke. On and on the time dragged uncomfortably, until I couldn't stand it any longer.

"Maxim, I didn't realise you had an interest in the fashion business." The way I'd blurted it out caused Brett's knife to scrape noisily over his plate. I didn't dare look at him as I kept my gaze on Maxim, trying to gauge his reaction.

One brow rose, the only sign that he might have been surprised by my question. "I've an interest in many things. Fashion is one of them, yes. Why do you ask?"

The way he spoke indicated he already knew the answer, but I played along for now. "Charlie received an email from Sak Way. After a quick bit of Googling, we realised it is a company you own."

Brett stilled at my side; his food forgotten as his fork floated mid-air while he stared at Maxim.

Maxim looked between us before he focused on me. "Brett mentioned on Monday about your business plans. Some of my business acquaintances were quick to give out their cards to him for you and Charlie to contact. I thought it best not to wait and, how do you put it?" His lips pursed for a second, "Miss the boat?"

It seemed like a very reasonable answer, but a part of me felt there was something else to it.

"You never mentioned on Monday that you were interested," Brett pointed out before I could question him further. "Why didn't you just give me your card to give to Guy and Charlie?"

Brett made it more than clear he'd not been involved in Maxim's actions, and I could have kissed him as he washed away any doubt I might still have harboured.

"What, and let my competitors know of my interest? Have I taught you nothing about business?" he answered gruffly but without heat.

The levitating fork lowered as Brett grinned at Maxim. "When have I ever shown any interest in business?"

Maxim's lips twitched. "Never." His gaze shifted to me and something akin to pride shone from his face before it was masked. "At least your fiancé has some business acumen. I'd feared for the future of my business, but now I think I won't need to worry as much."

A buzzing started in my ears as I clutched at the cutlery I held in my sweaty palms. What the ever-loving fuck did he mean—fiancé? I glanced sideways at Brett to meet an equally bewildered expression. His mouth opened then closed as colour bleached from his skin.

Speechless, I looked between Maxim and Brett. Maxim shook his head. "He declares he's marrying Guy, now they are both acting like they know nothing."

"Father," Brett groaned before he dropped his cutlery and buried his head in his hands.

Had he told his parents we were engaged? Why would he do that? I swallowed to wet my mouth and struggled to find something—anything to say. If I'd thought the tension was bad before, now it was like wading through a vat of treacle.

"It looks like you've jumped the gun, Maxim. I'm sure Brett, when he declared his feelings about Guy, said he was going to marry him, not that he'd asked already." Hannah, even though she clearly was trying to make things better, only made Brett groan louder.

Brett finally lifted his head. His cheeks were bright red as he met my gaze, his own full of apology before he looked away. "The night I came to dinner...the vodka...well, let's just say I have holes in my memory of that night. I'm not quite sure what we talked about."

Maxim's laughter boomed out and Brett's mouth hung open. My own lips started to twitch, seeing the funny side.

"Oh dear, what a mess." Hannah sounded distressed as the food was forgotten.

Worried about Hannah, I tried to reduce her distress. "It's okay. There seems to be several misconceptions going on here—"

"I love you, there's no misconception about that. There's also no misconception about the fact I do want to marry you," Brett declared to everyone, stunning me.

"I...oh...is..." I trailed off when my throat closed up. Emotions I wasn't sure how to deal with left me floundering.

Brett twisted in his seat and took hold on one of my sweaty palms. His earnest expression did little to help calm the pulse thudding dangerously fast against my sternum.

"I'm making a mess of this. I'm sorry. I know it's too soon to talk about getting married, but I want you to know it's what I want, in the future." He sighed before he pressed a gentle kiss to my lips as if trying to reassure himself and me.

"We'll talk about it later, without an audience." I whispered, then returned his kiss, hoping there would be no other shocking revelations I wasn't sure my heart could cope with.

Shifting to face his parents, my stomach clenched. I wasn't sure what I'd expected to see, but both only appeared to show affection. Sensing the evening could go one of two ways, I settled in my seat and made a show of picking back up my cutlery as I met Maxim's stare. "So, you're interested in fashion. What part of the business interests you most?"

CHAPTER TWENTY-THREE

Brett

Chloe's smile was bright as I entered the office with just enough time to get settled before my first client was due.

"Coffee, I need an infusion, please," I asked after we'd traded good mornings.

"Oh, did we have a late one last night?" Her brows arched as she grinned at me.

"You could say that. Guy spent the night." I'd mentioned Guy to her but not how serious I was.

"I take it your full appointment list is why you're working instead of spending the day with him?"

I nodded. "Unexpectedly having last Friday off scuppered any hopes of that today." I sighed and went on through to my office, my arse complaining all the way. I'd mixed feelings about what had happened last night and a part of me needed time to recover and regain my balance.

When we'd got back to my apartment building, Guy had remained silent. That was until we were in the safety of my apartment with the door shut, then he'd let me know what happens when you put him in an awkward position. My arse tingled as I sat, and my thoughts went over what had transpired.

As the lock snapped into place, I took a deep breath and turned to face the silent man stood several feet away from me. The evening, surprisingly, had improved after my father had so spectacularly outed my future proposal plans to Guy.

Was he going to mention it now we were alone?

His blond brow arched up as his finger beckoned me towards him, before he slipped off his coat and went to sit on the forest-green leather sofa in front of the large dark window.

As I stilled in front of him, he patted his knees. "I've told you before what happens to my naughty boy."

The air was quickly dispelled from my lungs as my cock pressed more firmly against the zip of my suit trousers. "I...ohh—"

"Strip," *he growled, giving me no time to figure out how to finish answering him.*

Although my cock had other ideas and gave us both an answer.

Was I going to do this? Hell yeah! *I wasn't into a Daddy/boy relationship, yet excitement ran through me at him again taking control. The age difference added a new element and ramped up my desire.*

My fingers shook as I did as he asked, with him watching me intently. I sucked in my stomach when I stood naked in front of him. He shook his head but said nothing as his gaze showed appreciation while it roamed my body before it lingered on my arousal. Pre-cum slicked the flushed head and bobbed in time with my pulse.

A tip of one of his fingers stroked over the mushroom head, collecting the pre-cum. He brought his finger towards his mouth then hesitated as he met my hungry gaze. Instead of sucking his finger he smeared his lips with what he'd collected, mixing it with his lipstick.

Convinced I was about to drool, I swallowed hard, causing him to chuckle as he took hold of my hand to tug me until his lips were a mere inch from mine. The scent of my arousal on him was intoxicating.

Guy's heavy-lidded gaze encouraged me to take what I wanted. Not needing any further prompting, I pressed my lips against his and moaned in delight as I licked the seam of his lips, tasting myself. I pushed my tongue into his willing mouth, sharing my essence. The seconds he let me take control were heady, until he took over. The moment he cupped my cheeks to angle my head and control the kiss, to deepen it, I was lost to him.

We were both breathless and gasping for air when he released me.

"Lay face down over my legs," he rasped in a sexy voice, ensuring I didn't think of denying him.

He helped to position me, so my cock was trapped between his clothed thighs. The brush of the material added to my torment as he gently stroked my backside.

"If you want me to stop, all you have to do is say stop, and I will." His voice was strained as his fingers kneaded my arse firmly, warming the skin.

"I will," I whispered, convinced I'd be doing no such thing.

The sting of his palm wasn't as shocking as the sound of the slap in the quiet of the room. I groaned and lifted my bottom to meet the next spank as warmth radiated through my lower body.

The burning sensations that flooded my backside as Guy alternated between both cheeks, left me gasping, my mind and body fighting against each other. One wanted it to *stop while the other wanted more, but which was which I would not have been able to say.*

His hot breath hit my naked skin as he panted, and I whined while I writhed against his thighs. My cock was painfully hard as it continued to brush against the soft fabric, but it wasn't enough to make me come. I hung suspended between pleasure and pain, unable to reach the pinnacle.

"I need more," I cried out as I thrust back. My arse was on fire, but I needed more, needed something to push me over the edge. Sweat beaded on my skin as the torment continued.

Then, as if he'd flipped a switch in my mind, I started to float past the pain and the intense pleasure took hold. The air in the room seemed to thicken when it touched my over-sensitive skin.

I mewled as Guy tightened his thighs and angled his hips so my cock brushed against the top of his boot, and then I was coming. I strained against his hold as he gave two final spanks to my painful arse.

"Oh, you fucker...shit...gods...so good," I mumbled past my dry lips as I shuddered several more times as cum splattered over Guy.

"You've made me all dirty. Now what am I going to do about that?"

"Here's your coffee. Mr Williamsburg is here; shall I bring him through?"

I worked to keep my embarrassment under control as my now painful cock throbbed. I leant forward, resting my elbows on my desk to make sure Chloe couldn't see my lap. *You're at work, get a hold of yourself.*

"Give me five minutes just to check my emails." When Chloe nodded, I congratulated myself for at least appearing to be in control.

I sagged against the seat as she walked out the office. When had I ever let a man bother me when I was at work? After a minute of thinking, I gave up. Never! I'd never let Nigel get to me at work, not once. Then why was Guy different?

I laughed at my own stupid question. The love I felt for him was different, he was different. He was my everything person. *Oh crap!*

Then what did it mean that he'd not talked about the reason he'd spanked me?

There was no time to worry about it as Chloe returned with my client and I put on my professional mask, hoping I could focus the way I needed to.

Bone-weary with tiredness, I opened my apartment door ten hours later and groaned at the scent of food. My stomach growled as I dropped my briefcase on the table by the door so I could remove my coat.

I'd taken no more than ten steps into my living space when Guy appeared from the kitchen. "Oh, perfect timing." He walked to me, looking just as fetching as he did last night, even though he only wore a pair of fitted black jeans and a striped polo top.

As he stopped in front of me, a hand came up and touched the side of my left eye, stroking softly. "You look tired, sweets."

I leant into his touch and shut my eyes. "It's been a day. And I'm knackered."

He chuckled. His warm breath touched my lips as my eyes opened and I stared into his loving gaze. "Go shower, put on something comfy to wear, and I'll plate up the Indian food I've made."

"That's what I can smell. It smells divine."

"Then let's hope it tastes the same." He nudged me towards the bedroom door. "Go on, you've got ten minutes."

I eyed his clothes. "Don't you want to go out tonight?" Although I was asking, a part of me hoped he'd say no.

"Sweets, I can see you're beat. And as long as I'm with you, I don't care what we do."

There was nothing in his tone or expression that said he didn't mean it, so I gave him a grateful smile. "I'll be ten minutes."

I was back with a minute to spare and found my dining table covered in an assortment of Indian dishes. "I could get used to this type of treatment."

Guy laughed. "I like to be creative, that includes cooking. I just don't always have the kitchen space to do it. My Mum didn't like that I made a mess, and at uni the kitchen didn't lend itself to anything more than putting stuff in the microwave." He shrugged as he pulled out a chair for me. "Dinner is served."

He gave a small bow that got me laughing. "I love you."

His sudden stillness was more obvious as he hadn't returned to fully standing tall. When he met my gaze, his was full of vulnerability that left me clutching hold of the chair he'd pulled out for me.

"I love you too...last night, did you mean what you said?" His voice was barely above a whisper.

Trembles ran through me as I carefully nodded, unable to speak past the large ball stuck in my throat.

"Do you not think it's too soon? We've only been serious for a matter of weeks."

I hated the uncertainty I could hear. "To be honest, Guy, I've never truly felt like this about anyone before. I can't say what's different about you, or why I know for certain I want to spend the rest of my life with you, I just do." Heat in my cheeks made it impossible to hide my embarrassment as I struggled not to fidget and hold his stare.

It was hard to pick up what he was thinking as so many emotions ran over his face, too quickly for me to grasp them.

The scent of food hung in the air, but it lay untouched as we continued to stare at each other. The time seemed immaterial as I waited for him to say something, anything to untie the knots that formed with his silence.

CHAPTER TWENTY-FOUR

Guy

All day I'd thought about what Maxim had mentioned and what I'd avoided talking about last night when we were alone. I'd needed time to process, and as Brett stared at me with fear in the depth of his eyes, he'd confirmed one thing. I felt the same as him. I'd never experienced the kind of feelings I felt for him. That, however, didn't get rid of my fear that it was all scarily quick.

Brett was older and more experienced, so I didn't doubt his feelings. He also didn't seem the type to say something if he didn't mean it. So where did that leave us?

"I'm scared." My lips clamped together as that was *not* what I'd intended to say.

I swallowed a sigh as Brett released his white-knuckled hold on the chair and he walked around it so he could wrap his arms around my waist. "I am too. We don't have to rush into anything. I just wish my father had kept his mouth shut last night—"

"I don't," I stated, effectively shutting him up. "We need to be honest with each other. I've given a lot of thought to what you said last night, and I have to ask. Did you tell your father you want to marry me to piss him off?"

On a shaky exhale, he met my worried expression. "I can see how you might think that, but do you think I'm capable of that kind of spitefulness?" He appeared to hold his breath as his forehead wrinkled.

Seconds ticked by slowly as I struggled to find the right words. "No, I don't believe you are. However, you were drunk and sometimes we do stupid stuff when we've had too much to drink."

"I'll give you that, especially as I have holes in my memory, but I was already aware that I'd mentioned to my parents about marrying you. My mother reminded me Monday evening what I'd said. Drunk or sober, how I feel hasn't changed. I was shocked that my father decided to bring it up and that he seems to be okay about it.

"What I mentioned about proposing last night, I meant it. That had nothing to do with my parents. It was solely to do with my feelings for you. Can we get that straight?" He buried his face into my neck, and I tightened my hold on him. "I love you, Guy. I want you to...move in with me," he said in a rush.

My head came up slowly. "Was that what you were going to talk about last week?"

He nodded.

My breath caught as my pulse took flight. Then reality struck, and my smile dimmed as I thought of all the barriers to moving to London. "It's quite a commute from London to Brighton. It will cost me a fortune in train fares. Then there's Charlie and all the plans for the fashion show."

There was something calculating about Brett's expression as he spoke. "You have what, four months of uni left?"

"About that, maybe a little less if I get everything submitted early. With Nanna and Rachael's help, we've managed to focus on other course work. For me, the final submission is the clothing from the catwalk show." My smile brightened as I recalled Charlie had organised a venue for us. "Charlie talked Griffin into letting us use the ballroom in The Worthington for the show. The lecturers have all been invited and agreed to the venue change."

I chuckled. "We might have bribed them with a room in the hotel for the night."

Brett matched my grin. "Clever, I like it. I hope I'm getting an invite."

"You don't need an invite—"

"Why don't I need an invite?" Brett sounded confused and his brow was deeply furrowed.

"If you'd let me finish. You won't need an invite as you're taking part in the show."

I could literally see the colour drain from his cheeks as his head started to shake. "No, I couldn't possibly walk down a catwalk. Are you mad, look at me?" He all but screeched at me.

Increasing my hold on him, I stared into his insecure eyes. "I am looking at you. You're beautiful. You will look amazing strutting your stuff down the runway. Charlie has made you the most beautiful outfit to wear. And you'll be in the best company as Nanna and Rachael are both doing the show too." I injected as much enthusiasm into my voice as I could muster because I was terrified about what mayhem they could cause.

When his brows arched and his eyes widened, I couldn't contain my laughter. "They conned me and Charlie, but I'm sure it will be fun. Please say you'll do it, for me?"

The heartfelt sigh told me I'd won, but I waited for him to say it before congratulating myself.

"Okay, but if I make a fool of myself, it will be your fault."

All thoughts of continuing the conversation about moving were forgotten in my excitement to talk about the plans for the show. "You'll be amazing. Let's eat, and I can talk you through what we're planning."

The following morning, after I'd showered and dressed, I went in search of Brett. We'd not continued the conversation about me moving to London and I'd woken to find he wasn't in bed. Was his mind as full as mine about what it would mean if I moved in with him?

The sound of his voice drifted down the hallway as I exited the bedroom.

"I'll need to ask him. Yep." There were more murmurs and a few more yeses before I reached the living room.

As I walked into the room, Brett was stood facing the window so I could look my fill. He wore a loose-fitting polo top in bright red and a pair of designer jeans that looked as if they'd been cut especially for his shape.

Last night, when we'd talked about the fashion show, I was again reminded about how insecure he was about his figure. He was very conscious of his soft tummy and his muffin top. I loved them, he felt real to me.

I was slim, but by no means was I buff. I'd dated men who spent a lot of time working out and they were more focused on their exterior image than the interior person. It was a real turn off, and why I'd gravitated towards men that weren't all about how much time they spent in a gym.

Brett was gorgeous, there was no denying it. He sparkled, but it came from the inside and made you want to be with him. I'd spent time watching him, and people naturally gravitated towards him because he was genuine.

As if he sensed my presence, he swung around, and his face lit up the whole room.

"Perfect timing. Luke is asking if we want to go to his for dinner tonight?"

If I was judging him correctly, then he wanted to go, so I nodded. "That sounds good to me." The rewarding smile said I'd read him right as he confirmed my agreement.

I'd met Luke and Scott at their engagement party, and I'd enjoyed their company. I was aware that Luke and Brett were best friends, so this was like a dinner where you hope your friends approve of the new boyfriend.

My stomach tightened a little as I walked over to Brett and kissed his forehead as he carried on confirming the arrangements for the evening.

His lips puckered as I went to step back, and I chuckled before giving him a quick peck on the mouth.

I mouthed, "Do you want breakfast?"

He pointed to the door then between us as he listened to whatever Luke was saying.

"Want to go out for breakfast?" I asked quietly and received a nod.

Giving him a smile, I walked back to the bedroom to quickly change into a pair of red leather boots and grab my winter jacket.

An hour later, we were having brunch in Thomas, the restaurant attached to the Burberry store on Regent Street. The place exuded warmth I'd not expected from a designer café. The gold-and-brown colour palette wasn't over the top and the place was elegant and smelt of delicious pastries.

Our table was tucked into a corner, so we had privacy to talk. When the waiter left with our order, I chewed my lower lip trying to figure how best to bring up Brett's suggestion of living together.

As if he'd read my mind, Brett spoke up first. "We seemed to get off the conversation last night about you moving in with me. Do you think it's too soon?" he asked hesitantly.

I sucked in a shaky breath and reached for the hand he'd laid on the table. "If I'm honest, it feels a little soon. But that being said, there is a huge part of me that wants nothing more than that." I held up my hand as he went to say something. "Give me a moment. As I mentioned last night, there are a few things I have to consider. Money, my course, commuting, then mine and Charlie's business plans to set up our shop in Brighton." There was something akin to apprehension radiating off him when I finished talking.

"They are all valid points, but...what if...I moved to Brighton?"

As he spoke, it was as if he were trying to work out a solution to all of the things I'd mentioned. "But what about your home, your business?" I asked, hearing the hope in my voice while my heart beat madly in my chest.

His fingers tightened around mine. "I'm sure I can find a space to buy or rent in Brighton to set up my office. And I noticed there are several lovely houses on the sea front for sale. I'm sure we could find something...together."

There was excitement and something I couldn't grasp as he continued to talk through all the possibilities.

Was this real? Was I going to wake up and find I was dreaming? The hand holding mine and the glowing face in front of me seemed real.

Could it be this easy?

CHAPTER TWENTY-FIVE

Brett

A s my phone flashed an alert to remind me that the fashion show was the next day, I struggled to work out where the last couple of weeks had flown off to. Not that I'd needed reminding, with my stomach in knots and a ball of panic that liked to choke me every time I thought about strutting down the catwalk.

I wasn't in the least bit an exhibitionist. Okay sure, I didn't mind attention, but this? This was something completely different to being stared at by a man that might be interested in me.

Dry swallowing, I packed the remaining few items I'd need for a two-night stay in The Worthington. With the fashion show being on a Wednesday, I'd cleared my appointment book for today and tomorrow so I could drive to Brighton and collect Guy, Nanna, and Rachael. Charlie was driving up with Griffin, and they were bringing the clothes with them.

The last few weeks had been a flurry of activity, with me driving back and forth to Brighton every weekend to help Guy plan for the upcoming event. And yeah, I'd maybe been more of a hindrance at times when I'd distracted Guy to play hooky with me, but we'd still managed to be ready for today.

There was going to be a run-through late this afternoon. Griffin had let all those taking part in the show have rooms in The Worthington for the next two nights.

Luke had been spitting feathers about how he'd had to move paying clients to other floors so that he could house everyone in the show on one floor, to avoid complaints if the students Guy and Charlie had picked got too rowdy.

From what Guy said, it would seem Nanna and Rachael were the ringleaders, so they'd been put in a room next to the ones housing me, Guy, Charlie, and Griffin so we could keep an eye on them.

With my travel bag packed and in the boot of my BMW, I was on my way an hour earlier than I'd planned because I'd been up early from the anxiety. Music filled the car as I headed down the motorway.

Sub Focus & Wilkinson sang about the air I breathe as I listened to the words. *And you are all that I need, you're my gravity. Pulling you in so deep, ooh you're the air I breathe.*

My heart swelled at the meaning those words held for me. Guy really was my gravity. He kept me grounded, but gave me the freedom to breathe, to be me. God, it was exhilarating and terrifying to have someone know you on a level I'd never experienced before.

Had I hidden myself for fear of rejection? It wasn't the first time I'd asked the question over the last few weeks, and my years of training ensured I couldn't avoid the answer either. I had hidden, but the feelings I had for Guy refused to let me do that any longer.

Things between my father and me, with Guy's assistance, had also been something I'd not been able to ignore. We'd all had dinner together twice since the first time. Guy wasn't easily intimidated by my father, so it made the time together much less stressful. To the point that my father was much more relaxed around me, something he'd not been for years. It was something else I had to thank Guy for.

My father had had several conversations about investing in Guy and Charlie's business, and I'd kept out of it. Charlie and Guy had asked for mine and Griffin's opinion, but we'd been in agreement. The decision should be theirs, but I was a little surprised when they'd accepted his offer and not Griffin's. That was until Guy explained that although Maxim was connected to me, he'd keep the business completely separate, whereas Griffin wouldn't be able to do that with Charlie.

What would happen when we got married and my father became his father-in-law? *Maybe he's not planning to marry you?*

The thought burst my happy bubble as my fingers tightened around the steering wheel. There'd been no more mention of marriage, but it was there in the back of my mind all the time. Was Guy not thinking long-term the same way I was?

A cold sweat filmed my top lip as I indicated to take the slip road off the motorway.

We'd managed to look at a couple of houses, but Guy hadn't liked any of them. Was it because he didn't like them or was there another reason?

Stop making trouble when there is none. I chastised myself and recalled how impatient Guy was about the time I spent in London away from him. A warm feeling replaced the anxiety in the centre of my chest. *He loves me!*

A big grin spread over my face as I quashed the negative thoughts and let the building I'd placed an offer on for my business occupy my thoughts as I travelled the familiar roads to Griffin's.

The building was perfect for what I'd had in mind for the move to Brighton. I just hoped Guy saw it the same way. The place could work not only for my office, but for Charlie and Guy's new business. The original building had been split into two separate parts.

One side had been a café with an apartment above on the second floor. The other part of the building had its own front entrance to the large shop that had been a clothes shop. The second floor had good-sized rooms that Charlie and Guy could use to design and make clothes. It was housed close to the beach and there was a lot of footfall in the area.

I'd got a little excited when the estate agent had rung me to say it had been listed. I'd made a special trip to Brighton last week in the evening, not mentioning my plan to Guy in case it didn't pan out. But the second I'd seen the building, I'd known it was perfect, so I'd made an offer straight away, knowing the location was prime and it wouldn't be on the market long.

The seller had accepted, and I was now awaiting the searches to complete, along with the full building survey to check it was sound before I handed over my money.

Would Guy be happy with what I'd done? Money was still something that we chose not to talk about. I wasn't sure why he said nothing, but I had spent a lifetime avoiding thinking about it. It had become a habit that my financial advisor wasn't letting me get away with anymore, now I'd moved it from the trust account.

It would seem my father and I had come to a truce over it after we'd both got drunk on vodka. My mother seemed to think he'd been impressed that I'd decided to give twenty million to charity. I wasn't quite convinced, but as I couldn't remember, I had to believe her.

I chuckled. Would he be impressed to find out I'd invested yet more money in the houses Griffin had for youths escaping their crappy home lives?

I'd thought about taking it a step further and buying my own properties for those who lack acceptance from their families and friends for who they are. The concept was in its infancy and something I needed to spend more time researching.

Right now, though, all I could think about was getting through the next two days and surviving the fashion show. That my parents were going to be there was extra daunting. I just needed to make sure not to fall flat on my face or something equally as humiliating.

By the time I'd pulled into Griffin's drive, I'd worked myself up into a fine mess over all the possible things that could befall me.

At the door, I sucked in a salty breath and knocked with a trembling hand. When Nanna opened the door a minute later and eyed my face, I sensed I was not hiding my fear.

Her brow quirked up. "You look a little green around the gills, are you okay, laddie?"

"I'm about to embarrass myself in front of god knows how many people, dressing in who knows what, while having my picture taken by a celebrity photographer. Of course I'm not all right!"

Nanna slapped my shoulder. "Stop being a drama queen. We'll have access to alcohol and that will calm your nerves. If that doesn't work, I'm sure I've a pill that might help."

"Dear gods, woman, whatever am I going to do with you? Nanna, you do not give anyone any pills. Do you not remember what you did to me?" Charlie shouted out as he came down the hall carrying a large box, his face flushed bright pink.

She glanced at him as he dropped the box next to the two others I now noticed. "Give over, Charlie boy. I did you the biggest favour. Griffin ended up staying to look after you." She dusted her hands together. "Job done, you caught yourself a chap, and a lovely one at that."

Charlie groaned and glanced at me. "Don't accept anything she offers you. She'll have you flat on your back before you can say boo to a goose." With that, Charlie spun around and headed back down the hallway, calling over his shoulder. "We're all in the living room packing boxes."

Nanna shifted so I could move past her, then she gave me a wink. "Don't listen to Charlie boy, I'll sort you out," she whispered.

The laughter was out before I had a chance to stop it at the mischievous light in her eyes. Some of the tension I'd held onto drained away as I matched her grin with one of my own. "I'll steer clear of the pills, but the alcohol, yeah I'll need plenty of that!"

Her hand disappeared into the pocket of the cream loose-fitting trousers to pull out what looked like a silver hip flask. She checked the hallway before she shook it at me once and the thing disappeared back into the pocket. "Don't worry, I've got you covered."

"You're going to get me into trouble, aren't you?" I said, unsure if I should make a run for it now.

"You bet your cute little arse I am."

Dear lord, what had I let myself in for?

CHAPTER TWENTY-SIX

Guy

Nervous excitement meant I couldn't settle, shifting in my seat at the end of the runway for the umpteenth time. Next to me, Charlie was faring no better. It appeared the only one not affected was Griffin as he held his large tablet and appeared to be reading something on screen.

His hand came out absently and he stroked at Charlie's leg before he intertwined their fingers.

Distracted by a cough that came from behind us, I swivelled around to see who it was. A wave of heat crept up my face as I met a pair of onyx eyes as they swept over me with a look of appreciation before they moved to Charlie and Griffin, who'd both stood.

"It's good to see you, Marcus." Griffin held out his hand to the man dressed all in black.

His trousers were designer, as was the shirt he wore. They both held an understated elegance that if I'd been unfamiliar with fashion, I could have mistaken for a lower-priced clothing market.

He took the hand in what appeared to be a firm grip, while a wicked smile spread over his far too handsome face. I'd the feeling he left a lot of broken hearts behind him. I'd read a little about him, and if I recalled correctly, he was currently single. He was gay and wasn't in the least bit worried about who knew that, even though he came from old money. His family were quintessentially British, but from what I'd read, he'd spent a lot of his childhood in America.

"Are you sure you mean that? The last time we met, you threatened me." His voice was deep and masculine, with a sexy twang. He had to be around six-foot-three as he could easily meet Griffin's hard stare.

I tensed as I recalled Charlie telling me about the kick-off between Griffin and Marcus at the fashion shoot months back. Was it going to fuck things up for the fashion show?

"You had your hands on *my* Charlie," Griffin explained, as if that was reason enough to threaten someone.

Marcus' smile seemed to get bigger as Griffin dropped his hand. "That I did, but you can't hold that against me...it was work."

"Fuck off!" Griffin announced loudly as Nanna appeared on the catwalk.

"What's going on here?" she demanded, standing at the end of the runway staring down at us, her hands on her hips.

"It's nothing, Nanna, Griffin is just being silly. Nanna, I'd like to introduce you to—"

"Marcus Crestwell. Oh, now I didn't realise what a hunk you were," Nanna said in a voice that sounded sugary sweet and made me cringe.

Charlie rolled his eyes and muttered under his breath, loud enough for me to hear, "Oh, here we go!"

Marcus turned his attention to Nanna and reached up a hand for her to take hold of. She fluttered her eyelashes, and I swallowed the giggle that bubbled up when Charlie nudged me in the ribs.

"It's nice to meet you..."

"Agnes, I'm Charlie's Nanna. And I'll be one of the models you'll be photographing tomorrow. Now, we need to have a chat about this because I want to make sure you get my good side."

"Nanna, what did I say?" Charlie ground out, sounding all kinds of frustrated as he walked to the stage.

"Shush, Charlie boy," Nanna moved her gaze to Marcus and ramped up the smile, "Marcus won't mind a little direction, will you?"

I couldn't see Marcus's expression, but I could see his shoulders shaking. When he answered, his voice was full of laughter. "I love a bit of direction, Agnes." He released her hand, and in a flash, vaulted up onto the stage. "Tell me what you have in mind."

Charlie released a snort as Nanna gave him a look of triumph whilst taking hold of Marcus's arm and leading him back to the beginning of the runway.

Griffin placed his hand on Charlie's arm as he was about to follow. The smile he wore was tantamount to evil as he shook his head. "I'm sure Marcus will be fine, and if not, he'll get what he deserves for winding people up."

"Seriously, this is Nanna we're talking about here. She'll have him agreeing to all sorts if we're not careful."

The panic in his voice was catching as I followed his stare to where Nanna was now standing pointing at the rows of seats that lined one side of the runway. The dark blue and gold chairs had been picked to go with the navy and gold backdrop curtains we were using to arch the entrance to the catwalk.

We'd opted for the navy and gold thread as most of the clothes were bright and bold, so we'd needed a backdrop that didn't detract from them. The hotel had been accommodating, or should I say Griffin, adding additional lighting above the stage so when the models walked down the long runway, they'd be in constant light. The rest of the room would be in darkness so the full focus would be on the models.

Brett had baulked earlier, when he'd seen the length of the stage and the way it was lit up before he'd gone to check out the changing room. He'd been more than a little nervous, and I'd not missed hearing his little meltdown with Nanna when he'd arrived in Brighton.

The little detour Nanna had insisted on so she could grab supplies from the hotel room had given me time to distract Brett. Several kisses had helped to change the look of panic he'd worn to desire, which had lasted until we'd come into the ballroom that Charlie had picked for us to use.

Brett materialised a second later, as if he'd known I was thinking about him. His panicked stare met mine and I worried he looked a little too pale. He didn't get more than a few steps towards me before Nanna stopped him. I could hear her voice as she introduced him to Marcus.

From a distance, I couldn't quite make out the expression on Marcus's face, but there was something about how he stood a little taller as he reached for Brett's hand that got me vaulting the stage, much like Marcus had a minute earlier.

There was the sound of laughter coming from Charlie, which I ignored as I quick-timed it towards my man. By the time I got to them, Brett was flushed and stuttering. "Oh, don't be silly. I could never be mistaken for a professional model."

I slid my arm around his waist and tugged him against my body in a possessive move I'd have kicked anyone's arse for doing to me, but right then, all I wanted to do was ensure this man understood Brett and I were an item.

Brett accepted my touch and fitted his body into mine the way I loved. "Did you hear what Marcus said?"

I shook my head, even though I had a good idea, judging by what Brett had said.

"He thought I was a professional model." Brett's voice was high and breathy as he glanced between me and Marcus.

"You're beautiful sweets, how many times have I told you?"

He sighed, but looked more than a little pleased by my answer, his eyes sparkling.

"You're my boyfriend, you're biased. I don't think that counts."

Nanna tutted. "Less of that nonsense. Guy is right, you're a gorgeous boy, and if you were twenty years older, and straight, I'd be all over you."

"Oh…well…yes…lovely…thank you, Agnes," Brett stuttered, to the point I had to pinch my lips closed to stop them trembling with laughter.

"You, Agnes, are a hoot. I thought this was going to be a boring photoshoot, but now I think it's going to be anything but that," Marcus declared as his gaze swept over us, then went to Charlie and Griffin, who were still standing where we'd left them.

"So nice of him to attend our boring little photoshoot, don't you think?" I muttered to Brett as Marcus walked away.

That evening, Marcus's words came back to haunt me as we did the first run-through. The man in question was roaming the room with a camera clutched in his hand, paying no attention to the chaos that surrounded him.

"Nanna, you need to remember to keep in time to the music. There has to be a twenty second gap between you and Louise. She has to have time to reach the end of the runway, stop and give two twirls before heading back to you. You should pass about a foot from the end of the runway," I reiterated for the tenth time.

Her hands went to her hips as she eyed Louise. "Can't you walk a bit faster?"

Louise's face was full of laughter. "Agnes, if I go faster, no one will see the gorgeous designs Charlie and Guy have created." Louise was a second-year student doing sciences, who had been three doors down from us in the student digs. She shared a room with Kirsty, who had also agreed to be part of the show for us.

They were both game for a laugh and didn't take themselves too seriously. We'd wanted real people of all shapes and sizes. *Don't forget all ages!*

"You do know I'm old and have a dodgy hip?"

"Agnes, give over," Louise choked out, past gales of laughter.

Agnes stared at me and shrugged her shoulders. "I like her."

"Yes, she's great. But we need to figure out a way to get you to slow down."

When, several hours later, I made it back to the hotel room, I considered if I should have checked myself in for a mental health assessment. "I have to be out of my mind to have considered doing a fashion show to showcase my final design pieces."

Brett paused in stripping off his shirt, leaving it hanging open as he came to me and wrapped his arms around me. His naked chest pressed against me and the faint scent of sweat mixed with his aftershave. His eyes gleamed in the lamp light with a look of adoration that left me breathless

"It will all be fine tomorrow, you'll see. Everyone will be wonderful. The clothes I've seen look amazing and you'll pass your finals with flying colours." His voice was full of confidence before his mouth closed over mine. His hand stroked up my back and all my worries fled as I took control of the kiss, making him moan into my mouth.

CHAPTER TWENTY-SEVEN

Brett

All the confidence I'd felt the night before when I'd strutted up and down the catwalk like a damn peacock fled at the sight and sounds of the full room.

The day before it had only been the chosen models and a few of the hotel staff that had come to help make sure we had everything we'd needed. Now, as I peeked into the room, it was at capacity and filled me with icy dread.

Sweat gathered on my top lip and the confidence I'd had when I'd seen the outfit Guy and Charlie had created for me disappeared at seeing my parents in the front row. Beside them were several familiar faces, unfortunately, they included the dick, Blake Masters. Charlie had mentioned that the modelling firm he worked for had bought tickets to come and give him moral support. I suspected Blake had only come in the hopes that tonight would be a disaster.

"Come away from the curtain," hissed Guy.

"I can't do it, I can't. There are hundreds of people out there," I whispered fretfully, doing as Guy instructed.

He didn't get a chance to reply as Agnes appeared next to him and took hold of my hand in a firm grip. "Come with me. Don't worry, Guy, he'll be fine." With that she whisked me to the back of the large room we were using as a changing room. The last thing I saw was Guy's worried frown.

When we got to the chair where I'd laid the outfit I was going to wear, Agnes stopped. "Here, face the wall like you're going to undress." She gave a furtive look around before out came the hip flask. She made quick work of unscrewing the top before giving another quick glance about. Seemingly happy no one was watching us, she handed it to me. "Take a good nip."

My empty stomach rebelled at the thought of drinking when I'd not eaten because I was too nervous, but my head wasn't in the least bit concerned about that right then. I took a big gulp. I choked as the pure alcohol seared the back of my throat and spread through my body like a burning wildfire. It stole my breath, and I was convinced I'd killed about ten thousand brain cells as it flooded my head.

"Holy mother…what…is that," I coughed out, while struggling to take a breath.

"Don't you be worrying your pretty little head about what it is. Let's just say, it's premium stuff."

"Premium? I think it's just removed my stomach lining and killed a few million brain cells." As I spoke, the alcohol started to take effect, and I felt way more relaxed than I had a few seconds ago. "Shit, how can that already be having an effect?"

"I told you, it's premium stuff. Here, have another swig."

With the effects of the alcohol combatting the nerves, I shrugged and did as she suggested. I took two big gulps this time. My eyes streamed, but the effects were worth the burning and the loss of brain cells.

Feeling more than a little floaty, I grinned at Agnes. "I think I should keep that flask just in case of emergencies." Was I slurring my words? No, I couldn't be.

Agnes shook her head, and I felt a wave of dizziness wash over me, causing me to clutch at her.

"Oh, I think I might have miscalculated. I didn't realise you're a lightweight."

"I'll have you know...oh, what was I going to say?"

Guy's voice broke my concentration as he shouted out, "We've got fifteen minutes to show time, time to get changed, guys."

I glanced at him and grinned. "He's so forceful," I said as I glanced in Agnes's direction, "all the time. Even in the bedroom."

Delight filled Agnes's face as she patted my arm. "Is that so, do tell."

"Agnes, now is not the time to be pumping Brett for information. You need to get changed, both of you," Rachael advised, appearing from, well I'd no clue, but I gave her a smile, then set to get undressed.

My inhibitions seemed to have disappeared as I stripped down to my underwear and cooed over the clothes as I redressed. By the time I had the chocolate brown trousers on and the suede boots to match, I couldn't remember why I'd been anxious.

When I got to the fitted, cream shirt, my fingers didn't seem to want to work. After several attempts, Rachael was howling with laughter as Agnes came to my rescue. She managed to get me into the boned waistcoat.

As I stood in front of the mirror to examine myself, emotions filled my chest and a lone tear slid down my cheek.

The waistcoat was a thing of beauty. The deep chocolate brown was off-set with panels of cream satin and topped with lace. It hugged my body and made my waist appear tiny as it cinched it in. The trousers tapered in at the bottom and I'd pushed them into the boots. It gave me a chic appearance, one I'd have avoided normally, thinking I'd look too pretentious.

I'd had my hair cut and I'd styled it back off my face. The alcohol had given me a nice glow. "I look hot!" I announced, rather loudly it would appear, when several heads turned and I caught faces in the mirror.

"You do. Wait till Guy gets a load of you, he'll cream his pants," Agnes stated in a voice filled with devilment.

"That would be such a waste."

Rachael choked and coughed, while Agnes snorted with laughter.

"What? It would be." I turned to face both women, who looked equally as stunning. Agnes wore a beautiful kaftan style dress in a rainbow of colour, all in geometric print. Her hair sat around her face in tousled curls and light make-up gave her a youthful appearance.

Rachael's choice of top in cerise with colourful flowers was matched with black, loose-fitting silk trousers. Her normal puffball hairstyle was replaced with a chic cropped style that feathered onto her face.

Guy had such an eye for what suited a person.

I puffed up with pride as I hooked out my elbows. "Are we ready to wow them, ladies?"

Agnes had her back to the room and the hip flask appeared from under the folds of the long silky kaftan. She gave me a quick wink as she wiped the top of the flask taking a sip, then handing it to Rachael. She followed what Agnes had done before offering it to me.

"No, he's had enough," Agnes argued with Rachael.

But it was too late as I'd already snatched it out of her hand. Before she could stop me, I took a deep swallow, hardly feeling the burn this time. "This stuff...it's strong."

"Yes, it is, so that'll be enough for you." The flask was taken out of my hand quick as a flash before I could contemplate if I needed a little more. The floaty feeling was really starting to kick in.

"Get a shifty on, you're on in two minutes," Louise specified as she checked her watch, walking towards the curtain hiding the stage from our view.

My legs felt a little like rubber as I walked with Rachael and Agnes to stand in the line of people chatting nervously in front of us.

The buzz was back in my head, but I wasn't sure if it was nerves or the alcohol. I didn't get a chance to figure it out as we moved forward towards the curtain and closer to a harried-looking Guy.

"My man looks a little stressed, maybe you should offer him some of your secret potion."

When I met Guy's gaze, I gave him a reassuring smile.

His eyes seemed to get incredibly wide before he glanced at Agnes and mouthed something I couldn't quite make out.

Agnes lifted her shoulders but said nothing, so I thought I must be mistaken.

A minute later, I was standing next to my man with the urge to kiss him. I cupped his cheeks. "I love you. Look, you made me look beautiful." Then I kissed him with all the feelings that had swam to the surface at seeing how I'd looked in the mirror.

He moaned and pulled back. His gaze wasn't on me when he muttered through what I thought were clenched teeth, "Nanna, I'm going to kill you."

Before I could pull my thoughts together to question why he'd kill Agnes, I was gently nudged towards the stage. The curtains parted, and for a second I was blinded by the lights before I remembered what I was supposed to be doing.

Blinking away the white spots, I sauntered out onto the stage, stood for what I hoped was the allotted time, then tried to walk slowly and confidently down the runway as Guy had taught me.

My hips seemed to have a mind of their own, so I went with it as they moved in time to the sexy music thumping through the speakers. By the time I got to the end of the runway, I was having the time of my life. I couldn't remember why I'd been in the least bit worried.

I gave the crowd a smile I hoped looked as sexy as it felt, then swirled around to show off the outfit. Only, I forgot which way I was supposed to be turning. My foot caught on the edge of the runway and before I could right myself, I lurched headfirst into the crowd.

The only thought I had as my arms flailed was, 'please don't let me squish a lady'.

CHAPTER TWENTY-EIGHT

Guy

As I watched Brett like a hawk as he swayed to the beat of the music and sashayed down the catwalk, my heart was full of love. He looked utterly stunning as the lights caught the flecks of gold in his hair.

When I'd had Charlie create my waistcoat design for him, I'd figured he'd look good, but he was breath-taking. The outfit seemed to take away his body consciousness issues. Or maybe that was whatever Nanna had given him. His glassy-eyed expression and over exuberant behaviour hinted that he may have been Nanna-ed!

Louise nudged me, and I nodded to her to step onto the stage, but I kept my gaze on the man who stopped just shy of the end of the runway. I couldn't see his face, but he stood proud and had cocked his hip. Then, as Louise started to walk down the runway, the air got stuck in my lungs as Brett twirled in the wrong direction. His arms came out but to no avail, and he teetered off the end of the stage, headfirst into the front row of the crowd.

There was a collective gasp and people seemed to move away from the end of the stage as my mouth worked but no words came out. The pulse pounding in my ears deafened me to everything as I darted down the side steps, past the other models, and ran out the door that led into the ballroom.

Panic gripped me by the throat that Brett might have injured himself or someone else, and I'd get sued. Did the hotel have insurance?

The bubble of hysterical laughter caught in my throat as I darted past the people who had stood to see what the commotion was. There were several people stood in my line of vision, so I didn't immediately see Brett.

I shoved through the crowd and my throat constricted at the sight of Brett grinning up at Blake Masters, who it appeared he had landed on. A jealousy I wasn't used to slid greasily in the pit of my stomach as I came to halt while my hands were reaching for Brett.

"There's just been a little mishap, please can everyone take their seats. The show must go on and all that jazz," came Nanna's voice over the microphone.

There were collective titters of laughter that I ignored, along with Nanna, my attention fully on Blake and the hands he had on my man, that he didn't show any sign of removing.

"Brett, sweets, are you okay? Did you hurt yourself?"

At the sound of my voice, Brett shifted and attempted to sit up, his glassy eyes meeting mine. "This thoughtful man caught me."

The accompanying smile he gave Blake caused my teeth to grind together. "That was very kind of him," I said through gritted teeth as I met Blake's smug smile. "But let's get you up and back behind the stage to check you're okay."

"Alrightttttyyy," he sing-songed as he flailed a little more before managing to get up. People all around him laughed, even his father.

It took several minutes to get him back behind the curtain, while the show carried on as if nothing had happened.

Brett let me guide him to a chair before he offered up his lips for a kiss, appearing none the worse for wear after his tumble off the stage. "Kissy. I deserve a kissy after rocking it out there." He sucked his lower lip in between his teeth, his face wearing a slightly befuddled expression. "Or I think I was before I fell."

I was unable to hold back the laughter as he pouted at me. "You were amazing out there. Now tell me, what did Nanna give you to help relax you?"

His eyes gleamed and he shrugged. "Premium stuff. Three...or was it four mouthfuls? Anyway, it doesn't matter, it was good stuff, you should try it."

He was being utterly adorable, but the anger I felt at Nanna giving him...whatever she'd given him, remained. The sounds of the full room faded as I caved and gave him the kiss he wanted, and that I needed to reassure myself he was okay.

The taste of alcohol was tempered with Brett's sweet taste as he opened and groaned into my mouth. His hands came up and clutched at my shoulders as I swept my tongue deep into his mouth.

It took seconds to register the sound of clapping and I remembered where we were. The moment I released Brett's lips he complained, and even though I was tempted to kiss him again, I refrained as it struck what I was supposed to be doing.

"Guy, come on, we need you on stage," Charlie called.

Brett stood, swayed, then righted himself before he held out his hand. "Come on, your fans are waiting."

I chuckled as I intertwined our fingers. "Just don't fall over this time."

We managed to get through the last run-through with everyone on stage and me walking Brett down the catwalk. There were several cheers when we got to the end without further incident. I didn't fail to miss how Blake was eyeing Brett as we stopped and bowed to everyone.

Back in the changing room, Marcus came in. His presence caused a stir as people stopped talking to watch him stride to me.

His face was alight with pleasure. "I managed to get what I think will be some amazing shots. Do you mind, once I've developed them and you've approved them, if I use some in my next book?"

Brett clutched at my hand. "What an amazing opportunity to show off your designs."

I gave Brett a huge grin before I glanced back at Marcus. "What he said, and just, wow! That's a seriously generous offer." A wave of warmth rode up my neck as Marcus gave me a look I couldn't begin to interpret.

"You've a real talent, you *and* Charlie. You've not followed tradition, and using real people was pure genius because it shows how accessible your designs are to everyday people. Not just those wire-thin models that aren't a true representation of the public."

The warmth in my face went from a comfortable three, to an inferno ten at his compliments. "Clothes should be designed for real people."

He gave my shoulder a pat, then he smiled at Brett. "I'll make sure to keep the pictures of you tumbling off the stage for Guy's eyes only."

He chuckled when Brett released my hand and buried his face in his hands, mumbling, "I'm going to kill Agnes, mark my words."

"You'll need to get in line," I growled, sweeping my gaze around the room to find the culprit. "Where did she go?"

Marcus pointed towards the door where the after-show party was about to happen. "In there."

"Are you up for mixing for a bit?" I looked directly at Brett who, thankfully, was no longer hiding.

"I think so, as long as I stay clear of alcohol." He shook his head and licked his lips. "Although I've a feeling it wasn't just alcohol in Agnes's hip flask."

The resignation was tempered with humour as he took the hand I offered.

"That women should come with a warning label," Marcus said, apparently unable to get his laughter under control.

Brett sighed mournfully. "I think you're right."

"She at least made amends by keeping the show going, so there is that," Charlie muttered as he came to stand next to Brett, looking him up and down. "I'm so sorry. I've had a little chat with Nanna. She'll be giving you both a full apology. It appears she mixed several spirits together to make a concoction to help relieve everyone's stress."

I bit my lip, but Brett, who was still under the influence of that concoction, roared with laughter. "That will teach me."

"Yeah, well, she's lucky I don't send her back to Scotland." The look on his face made it perfectly clear just how serious he was, so I kept quiet as we started to follow those who'd participated in the runway show into the other room. We'd decided to hold a thank-you party for all involved and for those who'd decided to buy a ticket to attend the show.

Charlie had invited some well-known fashion experts and writers from fashion magazines in the hopes of creating some buzz. I'd seen Maxim had invited several influential businessmen too. I'd recognised a few of them from the search Charlie had done when Brett had given us their business cards.

After much toing and froing, we'd opted to just go with Maxim as an investor in the business, for now. I'd had some worries about that, but I'd kept to myself for the time being. The memory of our first encounter in the hotel hallway liked to come and do a sneak attack when I wasn't feeling confident we'd succeed.

"Do you want a drink?" Charlie asked as we stopped at the bar, situated on the left of the room. It was packed with people vying to get a drink.

Brett spoke up first. "I'll pass but take a bottle of water, please."

"I'll have the same, I want to keep a clear head in case anyone wants to talk to me." No sooner had I spoken, Blake Masters appeared through the crowd with three other men I didn't know.

I heard Charlie groan before he stepped into the busy crowd around the bar. With no chance to follow him, Blake's hand landed on Brett's arm and it instantly put my back up.

"Are you all right, Brett? You landed quite *hard* in my lap." His voice was smarmy as his fingers trailed up and down Brett's arm.

The jealousy was back, and she was in a bitchy mood. I removed the small gap between Brett and I as he remained silent, looking far from comfortable. I tutted at Blake as I lifted his hand off Brett. "All that money and you still haven't managed to snare yourself a boyfriend, Blake? So sad that you have to resort to grouping mine instead."

A deep-red hue slashed across Blake's cheeks as his eyes narrowed on me. "I hear that you've wormed your way into Maxim's wallet. Sounds like maybe you are a gold-digger after all, Guy. Most people use their charm, personality, and good looks to win other people's affection."

The implication was very clear, and those around us gasped as Brett's whole body became rigid against mine. His mouth opened, and I gave him a little squeeze to indicate I was fine.

When he relaxed against me, showing he trusted me, I met Blake's pathetic stare with a smile I hoped was full of the love I felt right then. "Oh, I quite agree, I just thought it a bit mean to use what you don't have against you."

There were titters of laughter as I swept my gaze over him and shook my head before I led Brett away.

We didn't get more than a few steps before Brett pulled me up short. "I love you," he declared in a loud voice before he kissed me with a passion that left me in no doubt about how he felt.

CHAPTER TWENTY-NINE

Brett

The tip of my finger traced over the glossy photo Guy had couriered to my office that morning.

In the picture, I was stood at the end of the catwalk, before the incident I refused to think about, and for want of a better word, I looked…gorgeous. I was smiling directly at the camera, and though I looked slightly stoned, Marcus had captured the happiness I was feeling in the moment. The confidence that the outfit had given me…no, not the outfit. If I were honest, that confidence came from being loved by Guy. It was there in the breadth of my smile, it shone out of me.

When I'd got home an hour earlier, I'd searched through all the places I'd kept old photos to see if I'd ever looked that happy before. I'd quickly come to the conclusion that even in my drunken pictures with Luke and some of my exes, I'd never appeared this happy.

Oh I could put it down to the photographer, because Marcus was a true genius behind the lens, but the second photo he'd taken of me kissing Guy right after I'd declared I'd loved him was very revealing. And though it was only a side shot of us both, we wore mutual expressions of love and desire. He'd done some blurry thing with the crowd around us so it looked as if we were alone in that moment. The focus of the shot was love. The love I felt for Guy and the love he felt for me.

My heart skipped a beat as I rubbed at my chest. The picture captured what he truly meant to me. The first thing I was going to do when I got Marcus's number was to ask for the negative so I could have the picture blown up and framed for my wall. I never wanted to forget how Guy made me feel, not ever.

How can you when he sits inside your heart?

What I was sure was a stupid grin spread over my face until my cheeks ached. How the heck had I got so lucky?

As I recalled how crazy the last few weeks had been and the lack of time I'd had with Guy, my smile dimmed a little. It had been three weeks since the fashion show, and although things had calmed down now that he'd submitted his final pieces, he'd been ultra-busy sorting out the details of the business agreement with my father.

Then there'd been the flurry of orders he and Charlie had received, requests for interviews to talk about their design concept, even invites from fashion houses trying to entice them to join up, rather than going out on their own.

Guy was in his element, and Charlie was beside himself that he could finally give up modelling. The excitement I felt for them both cut through a little of my frustration at the lack of time we had together.

For some reason I couldn't solely blame Guy's busyness on, I'd not yet spoken to him about finalising on the building in Brighton. We'd put the house-hunting on hold as there was nothing new listed that intrigued us enough to go view them.

That left me in a situation where my weekends were becoming the whole focus of my week, and it was telling when Luke had started to complain that I was ghosting him. Guilt about it didn't sit well with me, so I'd rearranged my last client today so I could meet Luke this evening.

I glanced at my watch and cursed at the time I'd wasted searching for pictures. Leaving the photos on the coffee table, I got up to change for dinner.

With only a minute to spare, I entered the busy La Trattoria Di Amore restaurant and met Adam's warm smile with one of my own. "Good evening, Brett, it's good to see you again." Adam held out his hand as I stepped further into the warm, scented entrance.

The first time I met Adam had been a little stressful, to say the least! I had been meeting Luke for lunch at this restaurant, and he'd been an absolute shit to one of the servers, Scott. Adam, being Scott's best friend, had taken none too kindly to this, and wasn't afraid to make it known. A little later, it transpired that Luke was being a shit to Scott because he had feelings for him...go figure! Thankfully, now that the two of them were madly in love and Scott seemed to be happy all the time, Adam was prepared to bury those old feelings.

"It's been a while, I hope you're well." I glanced at Adam's ring finger and smiled as I shook his hand. "It seems you've managed to get married since I was last here."

His face morphed into an angelic expression that held me mesmerised. "Yes, yes I have. Carl, if you can believe it, is the most amazing husband, so thoughtful and loving," he gushed as his cheeks pinked adorably.

"I'm so happy for you."

He glanced towards the partition before he looked back at me. "Maybe Luke and Scott, now they're engaged, will be the next to tie the knot."

I chuckled. "You never know. Is Luke here?" I asked as I slipped off my overcoat and went to hang it up on the coat rack.

"Yes, he's here. Follow me and I'll show you to your table."

As we moved through the restaurant, all the tables were full. From what Luke had mentioned, he'd managed to grab a last-minute cancellation because Scott worked for the chain of restaurants. The scent of food was rich and appetising as I walked behind Adam. The music was something dreamy and matched the pink lighting that cast a warm glow over everything.

When Luke spotted me walking towards him, his tanned face lit with a smile. "Thank god you're here, I thought I was going to have to start eating the menu!"

"Keep your hair on, I'm right on time," I said without any real heat, before I thanked Adam for pulling out my seat and the menu he handed me before walking off.

Once we'd picked our food choices and a bottle of wine, I sat back in my seat and stared at my best friend. He'd never looked more relaxed or happy, that I could recall. It was as clear as the nose on my face how much of a difference Scott had made to his life.

I tapped at my lower lip before asking, "How did you know when it was the right time to propose to Scott?"

His eyes widened and his lips pursed for several seconds before he answered. "My best friend pointed out that I was a fool and should stop hiding, that's when." He chuckled when I gave him the finger. "Okay, I'll behave."

He sat forward, his elbows balanced on the table as his face became serious. "I can't say it was any one thing. I woke one morning as he was lying sleeping at my side, and when I looked at him, I found myself imagining what my life could be with him and what it would be without him. It was no contest. His love gives me something I didn't even know was really missing from my life. I can't explain it any more than that if you catch my drift?" He shrugged and shifted back, but his gaze remained on me.

"I told my parents I was going to marry Guy."

A look of alarm spread over his face. "Shit, how did that go down?" Luke was more than aware of all the issues I'd had with my father over the years. His own father hadn't treated him much better.

"I can't tell you, as I was pissed on Russian vodka, so I've no clue how my initial announcement went down. The second time, he seemed okay, remarkably. But I don't know if that was because he'd outed me to Guy by declaring our engagement."

"What? Hang-on, back up, you've lost me. Explain that to me again."

I shook my head as I ran back through what I'd said, then went on to try and explain what had happened between going to my parents for dinner and then taking Guy to meet them the first time.

"Wow, and you've not spoken again about getting married? Although I get maybe why, it is rather quick. At least Scott and I had been together months before I proposed."

I argued back, "That might be so, but you knew how you felt for Scott for a very long time before you even got together. Answer me this, if you'd acted on your initial attraction to Scott, would you be married now?"

His dark brows rose as he reached for the wine the waiter had brought minutes earlier when I'd been talking. He took a sip, giving a nod of

285

approval as he allowed the wine to linger in his mouth for a moment.

While I watched him, my stomach clenched in anticipation of his answer.

Once he'd set the glass down, he met my stare. "Yes. Yes, I would. I wasted so much time being a dick and not owning my feelings. It's one of my biggest regrets. I know I can't change it, but it doesn't stop me from beating myself up about it."

The following sigh was full of regret as he sat forward, his expression hard to read. "There is probably little I could tell you that you don't already know, with what you do for a living, but if I were to give you one bit of advice it would be, don't waste time trying to figure out what society deems as right and wrong. We can't pigeonhole how we feel for someone else. Do what feels right for you."

My fingers shook as I reached for my own wine glass and let his words sink in. As I sipped the wine, an idea formed in my mind.

"Oh, I know that look, what are you plotting?" Luke asked as a grin spread over his face.

I swallowed my wine and returned the smile. "This is between you and me, right?" I asked, though I knew the answer even before he nodded. "Do you know of any good jewellery makers?"

CHAPTER THIRTY

Guy

For two days now, my neck and shoulders had been held hostage by an uncomfortable tension that seemed to ride through my whole body, and it wasn't showing any sign of abating. Two days of Brett being oddly distant and non-communicative. He was still ringing me, but he wasn't talking about anything of note. It was like I was talking to a friend who I didn't have much in common with, and it was like pulling teeth to get any information from him.

"Will you stop moping about the room, you're driving me nuts," Charlie complained for the third time, as I continued to roam the living room.

"I'm not moping, I'm brooding. It's different. There is something off with Brett and for the life of me I can't pinpoint what it is. At first, I thought it was the picture I sent him three days ago, but I've heard from Marcus that he has asked for the negative so he can have the picture enlarged." The warm, gooey feelings that information had given me hadn't disappeared, even with Brett's odd behaviour.

If I were less confident in how he felt about me, I might have thought he was getting ready to dump me, but deep down I knew it wasn't that. Maybe it was work stress?

He would have mentioned it.

Was he worried we'd not found a place in Brighton yet? Could be, but would that make him clam up tighter than a bad mussel shell?

"Jeez, I can hear your mind grinding through questions all the way over here. Sit down for pity's sake. Brett loves you. Maybe he's just got a lot on his mind."

My gaze flew to Charlie and I pinned him with a hard stare. "Do you know something I don't?"

His gaze shifted to the phone he held in his hand way too quickly for me to catch his expression. My gaze narrowed on his shaky hand and tensing shoulders, so I walked back to where he was sitting on the large sofa.

His head remained down as he showed interest in his phone.

"What am I missing?"

"I don't know what you mean? I've no clue about anything," he muttered.

He sounded anything but convincing, so I pushed again. "What do you know? Come on, we've been best friends for the last three years, I know you. You aren't telling me something."

As I stood over him, it seemed to take forever for him to meet my gaze. When I saw his guilty expression, I sucked in a shaky breath.

"Brett's bought a building in town for his business."

My legs turned to jelly as I took the couple of steps to the sofa, collapsing down next to Charlie. "Why…why didn't he tell me?" The hurt cut deep, but I couldn't think about it right then when Charlie masked his face and I again got the feeling there was more to this story. "What's going on?"

Charlie seemed to deflate before my very eyes. "I've no clue. He's in Brighton today to finalise the sale, why don't you go ask him."

I shot off the sofa. "He's in Brighton now? What's the address?"

There was resignation on Charlie's face, but there was also a spark of…I wasn't sure what, but the hairs on the back of my neck prickled with unease. Charlie recited a familiar address that, for a second, gave me pause as I recalled that part of the building Brett was buying had been a clothes shop.

My brows arched. "He's bought Jamie Lee's building?"

"Yeah, from all accounts she wants to return to the Netherlands to her family, so put up the building when the other tenants gave notice." He shrugged nonchalantly, but the tension coming off him told a different story.

A feeling nagged at me as Charlie all but put my coat on for me, then shoved me out the front door five minutes later while I was still trying to process what was going on.

The sky was bright, and the sun sat high in the cloudless sky, though there was little warmth to it. The air was crisp and held a tang of salt as I breathed deep to stem the fluttering going on inside my chest. It took me twenty minutes to walk to the address Charlie had given me. Any thoughts it would give me enough time to figure out what was going on disappeared when I stopped outside the building, as clueless as I'd been when I'd left Charlie.

Looking at the building objectively, I could see why Brett was going to buy it. It had curb appeal, was well-situated, with good parking nearby. The street was busy for the time of year, and in the summer the footfall could generate a lot of business for whoever took over the shops.

The way the building had been split, I could easily imagine Brett's office with a sea vista that his clients might find helpful to get them to relax. My gaze shifted to the second part of the cream building that had housed a clothes' shop I'd visited myself in the past.

I'd come to know Jamie Lee through Emma-Jane, one of the girls taking the same classes as me. Jamie was a bright and bubbly person who had a love for all things connected to the clothing industry. A part of me was saddened that she'd decided to give up what I thought was a lucrative business.

I sighed, at the same time pleased that Brett had found a base in Brighton. Why hadn't he mentioned this to me?

With no answer, or not one that I wanted to think about right then with uncertainty dogging my heels, I went to the main door of the first part of the building and knocked.

Several minutes later, with throbbing knuckles, I walked to the other side of the building where Jamie Lee's shop had been and peered through the windows. Or at least I tried to, but they'd been covered in white, making it difficult to see inside. Was Brett here?

Why hadn't I asked Charlie what time Brett was supposed to be here signing...I frowned. Would Brett come here to sign paperwork? I shook my head. Had Charlie got mixed up?

About to pull out my phone to call Charlie, the door to Jamie Lee's shop opened and there stood Brett, offering me a shy smile. "Hey you."

"Hey yourself," I answered, suddenly feeling awkward as I got a good look at him.

His suit was expensive, and the cut fit him perfectly. The chocolate-brown matched the waistcoat I'd gifted to him. It made me suspect he'd had the suit designed to go with it. The shirt beneath was cream and the top two buttons were open, revealing his throat. His pulse was visible, and it seemed to bounce excitedly against his skin.

Without saying another word, he took a step back and held open the door in invitation. I sucked in a shaky breath and moved past him.

A throbbing started in my head as my eyes widened and I stopped just inside the shop. The sound of the door shutting seemed to fade into the buzzing in my ears as my gaze swept the table and two chairs sat in the middle of the otherwise empty room.

The table held a crisp white tablecloth, that was covered with sparkling glasses, gleaming cutlery, and what appeared to be a picnic lunch. The napkins were white, sitting beside black place settings. In the centre of the table was a bottle of champagne in a wine cooler.

Licking at my dry lips, I moved my gaze to the silent man standing at my side, watching me with a guarded expression. "What...why...celebration?" I stuttered, my brain moving too fast for me to catch up.

He chuckled, though the lines on his forehead deepened. He seemed to take a second to gather himself before he carefully got down on one knee.

Holy mother of god!

Was he—proposing?!

CHAPTER THIRTY-ONE

Brett

When my phone had rung thirty minutes earlier, and Charlie had informed me Guy was on his way, I'd struggled not to flee in panic.

Two days of running around trying to make today perfect had left me as nervous as a virgin on their wedding night. Guy's hurt expression when we'd ended our calls over the last couple of days hadn't helped to quell my growing anxiety that I wasn't going to make a massive fool of myself

But now, as he stood in front of me, I knew without a shadow of doubt that whatever his answer was, for me, this was the right decision.

He's going to say yes, he is.

The voice in my head didn't sound as confident as I'd have liked as Guy looked from the table to me and I slowly lowered myself to one knee. The varnished wooden floor creaked a little, breaking the silence as I held Guy's shocked gaze.

Please let me get this right.

Once settled, I dug into my trouser pocket and pulled out the small jewellery box. The jeweller Luke had recommended, whom I'd visited the day before, had thrown my plans of waiting a few weeks right out the window when I'd stepped into the man's shop.

There, in one of the glass-fronted cabinets, had been the perfect ring. The band was a black metal about a quarter inch thick, threaded with tiny, red garnet stones. The square-cut black diamond at its centre looked flawless and sat flush into the band. The white, red, and black all seemed to marry together perfectly, and garnet was Guy's birthstone. I took it as a sign, especially when it was the perfect size for Guy, and bespoke.

I'd all but skipped out of the shop, my head full of how quick I could make everything happen.

When I flipped open the lid and held the velvet box up towards Guy, his lips trembled while his eyes sheened with tears.

"The first time I met you, there was something about you that left me intrigued...and aroused..." I coughed to clear my throat as he gave a watery chuckle. "Well, you know the effect you had on me."

His eyes sparkled at me and my pulse fluttered madly as I inhaled and worked on what to say next without sounding any more like an idiot. *Good luck with that, you're not doing a great job so far!*

I swallowed a sigh and carried on. "The second time we met, I recognised the truth of your words about not being ready for more when we first met. All I'm going to say is that I'm grateful to the universe for putting you back on my path and, I suppose, my father for bullying me into coming on holiday with him when I really didn't want to."

This time his laughter was rich and full, and I joined him, the tension in the room releasing as the perfect words were suddenly right there. "I love you. I love you with all my heart and I want to spend the rest of my life showing you just how much you mean to me. I want you to be a part of my life in every way. Support you in your every venture." I swept my free hand around the room. "I'm sure you guessed that I don't need this space as well as the one next door."

His smile was beautiful as he nodded but remained silent.

"The second I saw this building, I sensed that this was ours. That it could be a part of the dream we could create together." I exhaled in a rush as my throat clogged and I had to swallow twice before I could continue. All the love I felt was there, waiting for him to claim it, and as I held his shimmering gaze that glowed with love, I jumped off the cliff. "Will you marry me?"

The seconds his mouth worked and no words came out felt like the longest of my life.

"Yes," he whispered as he dragged me up to standing and his mouth claimed mine in a hot, wet kiss. I felt it all the way down to my toes. The hand clutching the ring box went lax and there was a little thud as it hit the ground.

"Did you just drop my ring?" Guy mouthed against my slick lips. His hands roamed up my back to hold me against him before I could pull back.

"Yep, but I blame you. That kiss melted me from head to toe."

"Is that so," one of his hands moved from my back to slide between us. My eyes rolled into the back of my head as he stroked my firm cock. "This," he punctured the word with a hot kiss, "seems to be making a liar of you." Another kiss, and several strokes to my cock, and I was hanging on the edge of coming in my trousers.

"Please, if you don't stop, I'm going to come," I rasped past my tight throat as Guy refused to stop touching me. "I want to see what my ring looks like on your finger." The words were low and breathy as Guy's lips moved down my neck and I tilted my head to the side to give him better access.

"Is that so? Do you want the ring on my finger while I fuck you against the wall in our new business venture?" His voice was barely audible as his lips continued to press against my frantically beating pulse.

"Oh, that, yeah!"

I staggered a little as Guy released me and took two steps back, his gaze on the floor. When he bent to retrieve the small box, I was pleased to see the ring was still nestled in the black velvet. He offered me the box with trembling fingers. I took it and carefully removed the ring, placing the box on the table before I took hold of Guy's left hand.

"You're my heart and I will do everything to make sure I protect what we have." As I spoke, I slipped the ring onto his finger. The air trapped in my lungs at how perfect it looked against his flawless skin.

"It's beautiful."

A sob caught in my throat at the reverence in his voice. "Not as beautiful as you, but it's perfect for you."

There were no more words as his arms wrapped back around me and he kissed me with a passion that left me blind and deaf to everything but him.

Desperate for more, I tugged at his jacket as his hands roamed over me, pulling at my clothes.

I cursed my need to dress up when Guy, two minutes later, released my mouth and eyed my waistcoat with disdain. "I do love that waistcoat, but fuck's sake it's a real passion killer when you can't get the thing unhooked."

The laughter wouldn't be contained, and I roared as I struggled to help him unhook it. His impatience continued until I was naked, and I had a moment of doubt as he started to strip and I looked at the clouded white windows. Would people be able to see in the shop?

The thought fled as Guy stood naked and aroused in front of me. His gaze travelled down my body and for the first time, I didn't try to suck in my belly. The flushed desire I could see in his expression increased my arousal and my cock bobbed.

"Fuck, you're gorgeous. I want to eat you whole," he growled. He picked up his jacket and pulled out his wallet, inside was a condom and a packet of lube.

As he gloved up and made a show of spreading the lube up his hard length, a wave of heat spread up my chest at what was going to happen next. Any fear of being seen was lost under the need to have my—fiancé claim me as his. All my plans of having a romantic picnic disappeared under the blatant need etched into Guy's tight expression.

I took several steps back until I felt the wood-panelled wall against my skin. I shivered from the coolness. Guy followed and pressed his naked body against mine.

The next shiver that ran through me was for a totally different reason. His hot cock pulsed against mine as he ground against me, holding my gaze. "I love you." His hips gave a sexy swivel and I smeared pre-cum against his skin as lube spread over my lower groin. "I love only you, and not what you can give me—"

"I know—" His finger touched my lips, stopping me from saying more.

"People will look at us, the age gap, the different backgrounds, and they will assume, *wrongly,* that it's all about the money. I'll do whatever you want to make sure you know that is not the case."

With that, his lips claimed mine and whatever I was going to say was lost in the mind-melding kiss. It went on and on as one hand stroked up and down the side of my body while the other moved to my arse. The residual lube was slick on his fingers as they slid down the crease of my arse.

I parted my legs and he settled more firmly against me as the tip of his finger teased the sensitive skin of my hole. I shuddered as the tip sank in past the tight rim and the burn lingered for a second or two.

"So tight. Fuck, I want to sink into you so badly," he whispered against my mouth before reclaiming it, his tongue sweeping inside. It stroked against mine before he sucked my tongue into his mouth. He mimicked what he liked to do to my cock, all the while the tip of his finger remained just inside my arse.

I groaned in frustration and pushed down a little, hoping he'd get the hint I wanted more.

"Wicked boy." His eyes were full of desire as they met mine and his finger sunk a little deeper, the lube not enough to stop the pinch.

I didn't complain, I wanted to feel him. I wanted to remember how he claimed me with my ring on his finger. The primal feelings were well and truly in charge as I ground down and groaned when his knuckle dug into my arse cheek.

His nostrils flared and there were slashes of deep-red high on his cheekbones as he rasped, "You want me to make you feel it for days?"

I nodded, unable to speak past the lust in his heavy-lidded gaze.

His finger disappeared from my arse, but before I could complain he demanded, "Suck my fingers."

Oh, I could do that. The taste of my own musk and Guy caused a moan to rumble up my chest, speaking to how much I wanted this, not that my cock wasn't giving that away as it leaked all over Guy.

As he watched me, my cock throbbed and my arse clenched.

"Enough." The one word left me breathless as his fingers slipped from my mouth, leaving a trail of saliva on my chin.

His tongue followed the path before he claimed my mouth again. I gasped into his mouth as he slowly pushed two wet fingers inside me. The burn was there, but so was the pleasure as he slowly fingered me until I was mewling against his lips and bucking my hips.

Sweat slicked my skin by the time he spun me around and slid his cock into my arse. I was loose enough that all I felt was pleasure. The stab of disappointment at not feeling the burn was quickly followed by a wave of intense love that he'd obviously not wanted to hurt me.

"I love you," I panted breathlessly as his groin met my arse cheeks and his cock was fully inside me.

His fingers traced the sides of my face encouraging me to look back at him as he paused.

"You fill me until all I see is you. I love you so much." His hips moved in a sensually slow rhythm, his gaze never shifting from mine as he made love to me.

Time became unimportant as the love wrapped around us and I took what he offered. The rising tide of need hung suspended as he treasured me in a way I'd never experienced before.

My heart swelled, and yet more love filled it as his lips claimed mine in a gentle kiss that stole my breath and pushed me over the edge. I shuddered uncontrollably against him as he breathed into my mouth. "My love."

The world bled into a myriad of colour as cum pulsed from me and I felt heat fill my arse. Guy held onto me as we got lost in the moment and in each other.

When I recovered enough to get my bearings, I found myself sitting in his lap on the floor.

"This will be a story to tell our children," I murmured against his sweaty neck as I nuzzled closer, my brain still not quite back on-line.

My pulse spiked as it hit a second later what I'd said, but before I had a chance to say I was joking, Guy chuckled.

"That it will, but whatever you do, don't mention it in front of Nanna. You know she can't hold her water and I don't want to think about her telling your father, or Charlie for that matter, what we did here. I'm sure Charlie won't thank either of us for christening the shop this way." Guy sounded anything but worried.

I made a motion of zipping my lips before I grinned at him. "If I can keep the fact I'm worth billions secret, then I think I can keep this secret."

"That's because you're a reluctant billionaire. But that's okay because I don't love you for your money...I love you for—"

I pressed my finger to his lips and gave him a wide-eyed expression. "Not letting Agnes talk me into eating the chowder?"

He shook visibly, causing me to wobble on his lap as his eyes gleamed with laughter.

Whatever the future held, I hoped it was full of moments like this.

EPILOGUE

Brett

S at in my new office, I eyed my father across the desk. How much had changed over the last few months between us. The very fact he'd chosen to drive down to deliver some paperwork that could have easily been delivered proved how different things were.

He looked relaxed as he sat back in the new leather chair I'd purchased for the office as I'd left everything in my old office for the new tenant.

"Are you going to pop into the shop and see how Guy and Charlie are getting on with the set-up before you head back to London?"

His dark brows rose. "Is Agnes down there?"

His Russian accent thickened, and I clamped my lips together at the worry I could hear. My father still struggled with how to take Agnes and her suggestive comments. My mother thought she was a hoot, my father, not so much, when she flirted outrageously with him.

When we'd had dinner a few weeks back, and the vodka had come out, he'd finally confessed to the arse-kicking Agnes had given him in Switzerland at New Year. He'd laughed about it, as had Guy, whom my father had grown very fond of. They'd bonded over business, and somehow, his acceptance of Guy in my life made all the difference between us. It was only one of the very long list of things I was grateful to Guy for.

"You know damn well she is. There is no way she wouldn't want to offer her...advice."

"Pfft...advice, that's not what I'd call it."

This time a grin spread over my face as he rose from the chair and glanced at the door as if Agnes might burst in at any moment. "You off to make your escape before she finds out you visited and never went to see her."

My father's hand rose and he pointed at me, his face losing a little of its colour. "Don't you dare tell her I was here."

I stood as I laughed at the worry on his face. "I won't say a word as long as you look at the proposal that Griffin sent you for the new home for runaway boys."

He grimaced but nodded. I came around the desk and hugged him. His arms came around me and he hugged me back hard enough to make my ribs ache as he muttered, "Love you."

I didn't get a chance to answer as he waved me off and was out the door before I could blink twice.

I shook my head as I went back around my desk and shut down my computer. I locked away the documents that had been lying on my desk.

The document I'd mentioned to my father, that I'd been reading when he'd arrived, about Griffin's charity, would hopefully find themselves with a new contributor to help with their vision of creating homes for boys/young men in violent homes to escape from.

Griffin's upbringing had been anything but the lavish lifestyle he had now. I was privy to his past because he'd once been my client. Guy was aware I knew Griffin, but not about the fact he'd been my client. Although I suspected Charlie might have said something to Guy, it wasn't something I'd discuss. If Griffin wanted to mention it then that was his choice, not mine.

The only thing Guy did know was that I was a big supporter of Griffin's project and I planned to donate some of my time every week to the house Griffin was going to purchase locally.

Checking the time, my smile brightened, I headed out the office to see if I could entice my fiancé to take a break with me.

Guy

As I carefully tugged the silk top over the top of the hanger, I did my best to shut out the two women stood arguing over the placement of a mannequin. My nerves were already stretched to breaking point with only two days to go till the shop officially opened. The last three months had been a whirlwind of activity and change.

Last month, Brett had moved out of his London office, having rented the space to another psychologist he'd known for several years. This allowed for those clients unable or unwilling to travel to Brett to not be left without support.

It was one worry I'd ticked off my list, but there were still so many on there that some days I felt a little overwhelmed by them. Between juggling suppliers, setting up the utilities for the shop, advertising, and even the shop layout, it was all a bit much.

On the other hand, we'd still not found a house, so when Brett had converted the shop next door into his office, he'd had them renovate the apartment above and we'd moved in there.

My heart fluttered at the giddy wave of happiness that spread through me, that came from knowing that at the end of the day, I'd be going home to Brett.

I shifted to hang up the top on the cast-iron clothes rack, then reached to pick up another top sat on the counter at the side of me to start the process all over again.

Was money the root of all evil? It was a necessity no one could escape.

I rolled my eyes heavenward, recalling it had taken several arguments before I'd relented and used the money in my business account to refurbish the shop. Who gave someone five million pounds as an engagement gift? Maxim and Hannah, it would seem.

I sighed and rubbed at my temples, trying not to think about the money that sat in my business account. No matter how many times I'd tried to explain to Maxim and Hannah that it was a very generous gift, but way too excessive for an engagement gift, it fell on deaf ears. Brett was no help at all, agreeing with Maxim that the money would allow Charlie and me to focus on building our brand.

Charlie had kept his opinions to himself about it all, but I hadn't missed the gleam of mirth in his eyes when I'd told him what had happened.

Brett hadn't been much better, gifting me the deeds to the building. It had made the handcrafted bracelet in platinum, seem like I was...

Leaving the thought there, instead I shut my eyes and brought up the image of Brett's face when he'd opened the box and seen our names engraved into the precious metal. The guilt that wanted to take hold at only giving him a bracelet subsided. *It's not about money!* He'd loved my gift and hadn't taken it off since I'd given it to him at the party.

I was getting better at accepting that money wasn't what our relationship was about, though at times it was still hard to remember that.

Charlie just seemed amused at how I'd been played. How could I refuse engagement gifts without looking rude and ungrateful?

The volume turned up a notch and I spun around, glaring at Nanna and Rachael not three feet from me. "Jeez, will you two quit it? You're giving me a headache," I stated, loud enough to be heard over their bickering.

Did they take a breath? Hell no. The pair of them kept on going like I'd said nothing.

Why had I agreed to let them help me prepare the shop for opening? I glanced at Charlie, my brow furrowing as I recalled I hadn't.

I pointed to the two women, glaring at Charlie. "This is your fault, fix it."

"What! Why me? It's your layout they're arguing over."

His disgruntled tone caused me to tug at my already tortured hair. The last week had been stressful enough, putting together the shelving units and cast-iron clothes racks we'd bought. DIY was not my forte and it would appear it wasn't Charlie's or Brett's either, though they'd both given it a try. In the end, we'd had our arses handed to us by Nanna and Rachael who had no problem figuring out how to assemble everything.

That had resulted in them offering to help put out the display clothes on the old-fashioned mannequins I'd found in a junk shop.

Trying again, I called out, "Stop, that mannequin is going in the window."

Nanna glanced at me, her brow arched, and I braced for an argument. "Now, Guy, this mannequin would be best next to the door, especially with this outfit. It will encourage buyers into the shop."

My jaw clenched as I took a moment to collect myself, not wanting to let too much of my annoyance show. "If it's in the window that will have the same effect, will it not?" I asked, my voice terse and clipped.

Her expression turned thoughtful as she shifted her gaze to Rachael.

"I think he might have a point. It will also stop people pawing at it and possibly damaging it," Rachael added grudgingly, as she glanced about the shop.

I followed her gaze and the excitement that they'd tried to kill with their arguing returned.

The wooden floor looked like golden honey as the sunlight poured through the window. The mirrored walls reflected light, but also the clothes, so no matter where you stood, a strategically placed outfit would catch the eye. We'd gone for more of an antique feel rather than modern, clean lines that could be too clinical.

We'd purchased an old-fashioned tea service to offer cups of tea for those stopping to try on outfits. The changing rooms had been painted a soft palette of pinks and greens, and the chairs were velvet in the same colours. We'd also put down thick plush rugs on the floor to give a warm feeling to the space.

The second floor had been converted into three large rooms: one for sewing, one for meeting potential clients, and one for storage.

"How's it going?" came Brett's voice from the open street door.

I swung to face him and gave him a dramatic eye roll. "I hope you've come to save me from women who think they know best."

Nanna fired back, "Off course we know best. Didn't we sort out you and Brett?" At Charlie's laughter she pinned him with a stare that would have made a weaker man run. "You too, Charlie boy. If I hadn't got Griffin to stay that weekend, god knows how long it would have taken you to get your act together."

"Excuse me?" Charlie blustered.

Brett chuckled as he came and slipped his arm around my waist. I rested my head on his shoulder and watched the show. His fingers stroked up my side and a familiar wave of contentedness swept over me.

I tuned out the arguing and whispered, "Want to play hooky with me?"

Brett's head twisted a little to look at me, and a smile that could light the whole of Brighton spread over his face. "As your doctor, I think it's what I'd prescribe." He leant into me and whispered in my ear, "But only if it involves you and me naked."

Laughter rippled through me as I moved to take hold of his hand. "I think as you're *my* doctor, I should follow *your* orders."

His laughter joined mine as he tugged me to the door.

"Where do you think you're going?" Charlie called after us.

I glanced back over my shoulder and gave him a salacious wink. "To follow doctor's orders."

The silence that followed as we exited the shop lasted a few seconds before I heard Nanna shout, "Do you need an assistant?"

"Not in this lifetime," I called back.

The warm fingers entwined with mine tightened and laughter followed us as we headed towards our home. Could life get any better than this?

When Brett finished opening the door to our flat and turned to face me, his face shining with love, the answer was easy, *no*.

The End... Thank you for reading. If you enjoyed this book read on for an excerpt from The Light Beneath the Dark.

PROLOGUE

Lincoln

Bile rose up my throat as I entered the hospital and its scent invaded my senses. I'd only ever had bad experiences when I came into this place, and the hairs on the back of my neck standing up and my gut clenching, told me this time wouldn't be any different.

As I approached the front desk, the sound of my boots hitting the floor drew the attention of the sleepy-eyed woman who manned it. Her visible jerk and widening eyes were a reaction I was used to, so I kept my face a neutral mask.

"Can I help you?" Her southern drawl was filled with anything but friendliness.

"My sis called, she's havin' a baby. I'm her birthin' buddy." I rasped, and this time my lips twitched at the horror crossing the woman's face.

Her cheeks paled as her gaze roamed over me. I was sure she'd missed nothing, from my six foot five inch height, to the black leather I wore, to my long, wavy, dark brown hair I'd not bothered to brush in my haste to get here.

The call I'd gotten an hour ago from my sister to say she'd gone into labor early, filled me with dread. I'd somehow blocked out this possibility when she'd insisted on me being there for her. I'd been there for her throughout our shitty lives, and this was no different and she knew it. Even if I didn't have the first clue as to what I was doing. I mean, I'm a thirty-five-year-old tattoo artist who runs a motorcycle club. How the fuck was I supposed to be someone's birthin' buddy for fucksake?

"Her name?" the woman squeaked.

"Lizzie Stone."

The sounds of tapping filled the dead air between us and I scraped my booted foot on the floor as I glanced about, only seeing one other guy, slouched sleeping on one of the plastic chairs. A Tuesday in the hospital seemed to be a slow night. I'd have to remember that the next time I needed to come.

I hated sitting waiting for hours for some trainee to come and patch up whatever injury I'd gotten from fighting. They always gave me someone that looked like their Mamma still had to wipe their ass.

"It appears your sister is booked into the maternity ward, it's on the second floor." She pointed behind me. "Take the elevator to the second floor, turn right as you exit, and go straight down to the double doors. There's a bell to press to call for attention. They'll check with your sister before you can enter," she warned, and I rolled my eyes.

I glanced at the bank of elevators before giving her a nod. "Thanks."

In the elevator I rubbed at my eyes, trying to get rid of the tired feeling. I'd been up till one in the morning, finishing a tattoo on a prospect to the club. Quinn, aka Rattlesnake, had given me a headache as he'd whined and fucking moaned about how painful it was. Was it my fucking fault he'd chosen to have a rattlesnake tattooed from one hip bone to the other? I'd warned the stupid fuck it would be painful over bone, but he'd insisted.

I'd had a few moments of doubt, wondering whether we'd made a mistake giving him entry into the club the way he bitched, but he'd not passed out or asked me to stop, so that was something. Sid, my second in command and otherwise known as Serpent, had passed out cold the first time I'd tattooed him. He'd never lived it down, and the old crew still gave him shit for it.

The elevator chimed as it reached the second floor and, walking out of the elevator, I rolled my shoulders to ease the stiffness in my upper back from being hunched over. Turning right, I headed down the hall that smelled of disinfectant, though the scent didn't quite mask the odor of blood and guts.

The couple of people roaming the hallway dressed in dark green scrubs gave me a wide berth as my feet thudded loudly in the nearly empty hallway. The walls were painted a pale rose color and held some cheery pictures.

Reaching the door, I pressed the bell and waited, looking into the security camera.

"Hello, how can I help?" asked a tiny female voice.

"My sister rang me, Lizzie Stone. She's in havin' a baby. I'm Linc Stone, you should be expecting me. I'm her buddy to help her through this," I muttered, heat riding up my face at the silence that followed. I'd bet my last dollar the woman was probably comparing me to my tiny sister, with her angelic face. People often questioned our relationship until they looked at our eyes. The deep brown was threaded with gold and, depending on mood, could look more gold than brown.

It was the only good thing we'd gotten off our Pop. Mercifully, the mean ass fucker was long gone, so wouldn't get anywhere near this new baby to spread his hate.

"I'll need to check before I can let you in."

The tiny voice pulled me from a place I didn't really want to go and I watched the light above the camera go out. I stood like a dick, kicking at the floor. Why had I agreed to this?

The issue was, I'd do anything for my baby sister and she knew it. She had conned me when her fly-by-night ex had done a runner. What I should have done was chase his deadbeat ass down and hung him up by his balls until he agreed to support her. What did I do instead? Said yes to this madness.

That's why I'm here in the middle of the night, getting ready to tell her to breathe, and avoid looking at her pushing a tiny human out of her body!

What the fuck was I thinking?

Blaming the warmth in the hall for the sweat gathering around my hairline, I took off my leather jacket, leaving me in just the short-sleeved T-shirt I'd dragged on after the call. I glanced down and didn't get a chance to swear when there was a buzzing sound and the door was released. With a sweaty palm I opened the door, dragging in a deep breath to try and slow down my thundering heart.

The Killer T-shirt I wore was forgotten about as I walked down another long hall, this one in a deeper pink, past several open doors. Some rooms were empty, while others housed heavily pregnant women and what I assumed were their folks to help.

I pushed aside the fact I probably looked as terrified as some of the faces I'd seen. By the time I got to the desk, the one member of staff I'd seen initially as I'd started the long walk had morphed into five. I got the feeling whoever had answered the intercom had called their buddies to come and get a good look at me.

Belton, Texas has a relatively small population, around twenty-three thousand, and our motorcycle club is well known, if not for all the right reasons. It didn't stop the folks from coming to use the auto shop I owned to get their vehicles fixed, or to the tattoo shop I had to get inked. We paid our taxes and, on the whole, kept our noses clean...sort of. None of that made a difference to some of the folks though, who thought all bikers were just bad news.

I swallowed a sigh and tried to keep from scowling. "Lizzie Stone, where is she?" There was the sound of a loud mewl, followed by several cuss words I'd have been proud of, as a door opened behind the desk. Holy fuck, what were they doing to the woman?

Icy dread ran through me as I recalled Lizzie's insistence that I watch a few of the birthing videos on YouTube. The 'hell no' I'd stuck to might not have been the best idea.

What was I walking into? Right then, I'd have preferred running into a rival motorcycle club on my own, rather than facing what was about to happen.

"If you'll follow me, I'll take you to the birthing room. Lizzie has just been taken in. I'm Anne-Marie and I'll be the midwife assisting with the birth—"

"How the fuck can you be assisting if you're standin' here," I ground out harshly.

She took a step back, her face flushing rosily. "Erm…well…I was waiting for you," she stuttered, sounding flustered.

"Then you better get movin'." For some reason I couldn't explain, a sense of urgency took hold of me. I never gave the other women a thought as I met Anne-Marie's unprofessional glare.

"What're we waitin' for?" I raised the hand not holding my jacket and indicated she should get moving.

She swung around and huffed loud enough for me to hear, but I didn't give two fucks. The sense of unease I'd had from the moment I'd answered my phone was increasing by the second. I wasn't sure if it was just the reality of what was about to happen, or something else, but I'd always listened to my gut and it was saying 'get movin'.'

Anne-Marie led us back down the hall to a double door that required a security swipe to enter. The scent that hit my nose as we walked through was like nothing I'd smelled before, and I started to breathe through my mouth, not wanting to think about what it was.

We came to yet another desk, a woman in navy blue scrubs sitting at the computer. She looked up and I gave her ten out of ten for showing no reaction as her gaze swept over me, before going to Anne-Marie.

"Anne-Marie, I thought you were bringing Lizzie in?" Her tone was sharp and her eyes held a hint of steel.

"I was waiting for her brother. Stop fussing, Barb, I'm here now."

Something passed between the two women I didn't understand, but it felt off. I shook it off as Anne-Marie went to the door on her left and opened it. The cry of agony coming from my sister left me in a cold sweat and I was running through the door ready for battle. I stopped cold at the sight before me.

Anne-Marie chuckled and tapped my shaking arm as she passed by me, letting the door close behind her. "It's perfectly normal for Lizzie to be making these noises."

I didn't hear a word she said as I took in Lizzie. Her Stimpy pj top stopped at her bloated waist, revealing her bare ass. The back of the gurney she was on had been raised so she could hang on to it as she knelt. There were several sheets beneath her naked bottom half, covered in blood, and god knew what else, as it ran down her legs while she rocked, mewled, and cried out in distress. She seemed to repeat the pattern of rock, mewl, and cry.

The urge to run the other way was forced away by the need to make it all better, to stop what was hurting her. I felt utterly useless because this was a foe I couldn't fight. I threw my jacket onto a small two seater sofa in pale blue that was off to the side, taking a steading breath as I walked to Lizzie.

"Lizzie? Lizzie, I'm here baby girl, I got you." I avoided looking down at her lower body as I stroked her back as she'd taught me to do. Firm but not too firm. Her words ran through my head as she twisted to look at me.

Her eyes were full of tears and had black circles around them. Her skin was sweaty, and her long dark brown hair was stuck to her forehead.

"Oh thank god you're here. Help me Linc. Make the pain stop. Something's wrong, I can feel it," she cried, ripping at my heart with her anguish.

Her body rippled under my hand as I continued to stroke her. I glared at Anne-Marie, who was talking to the other woman wearing a set of pale lilac scrubs, paying Lizzie no attention. "Do something, she says somethin' ain't right."

"Now everything is fine. This is just part of birthing. The mom can get a little upset."

She got no further when Lizzie cried out, "I wanna pushhhhhh."

Anne-Marie came over and tutted. "You've only been laboring for a couple of hours. This is your first birth and it can take several hours before you'll feel the need to push."

Her tone sounded condescending to me, but as I was clueless, I bit my tongue.

But Lizzie was having none of it. "I'm tellin' you I need to fuckin' push," she panted, and took hold of my other hand, holding it in a death grip. "Make them do something," she pleaded with me after she got her breath back from another contraction.

Her whole body seemed to be alive the way it rippled and contracted. My knees weakened when I looked down between her legs and saw a pool of congealing blood. Back to breathing through my mouth, I glanced back at Anne-Marie, who didn't seem at all concerned.

Then all hell broke loose as Lizzie screamed so loudly I thought she'd burst my ear drums and the two women ran to the bed. Anne-Marie finally examined Lizzie and when she stood, her face showed real fear.

"What's wrong?"

She didn't answer as she hit the emergency buzzer at the back of the bed and people started to appear like ants coming out of the woodwork. They were everywhere. Lizzie held onto my hand, her eyes pleading with me to help.

"Can someone tell me what the fuck is going on?!" I roared to the room, my fear fully in charge.

The woman who'd been sitting outside at the desk stated, "We have no time to waste, the baby is stuck. The shoulders are wedged in your sister's pelvis, we need to get the baby out…" she trailed off as a man entered the room and she started to relay information to him, ignoring me completely.

I lowered my head to Lizzie's, my hair curtaining her face to keep her from seeing the chaos in the room. "I'm here, I'm gonna keep you safe, I swear." Even as I said it, I could see resignation fill her face with a knowledge I couldn't even fathom.

"Keep River safe. Promise me no matter what, you'll keep my baby safe. I've signed all the legal guardian paperwork and registered it with the court, so you won't have any issues." Her voice faded as her color drained. Her body went rigid and another scream froze my insides. This was followed by the cries of a baby.

"Come on Lizzie, you've got a baby to care for, stop this shit," I rasped through the ball of emotions clogging my throat. Her eyelashes fluttered and her hand went slack in mine.

ABOUT THE AUTHOR

Hi all,

My name is Jayne and I live in the Isle of Man. A tiny place in the Irish sea. It's an island steeped in folklore and history and just begs to have stories written about it, and one of my first inspirations. Over the last few years that has changed and now I find inspiration everywhere.

I'm an eclectic kinda girl so I've written contemporary and historical gay romance. I started with paranormal and I hope to go back to that in 2021, I'm also branching out in to crime, so let's see where that takes me. My head is so full of ideas, it could lead anywhere.

I hope you have enjoyed this book, and if you are in need of more, then you can find all my other books, on Amazon and in KU.

If you would like to give me any feedback or just have any questions, go ahead and friend me on Facebook, and I would be happy to answer anything. Well, almost anything. I hope you enjoyed this book as it was a little different for me. If you would also like to leave a review, then I would love to read your thoughts.

Thank you for taking the time to be part of my dream.